The
Georges
and the
Jewels

The
Georges
and the
Jewels

Jane Smiley

with illustrations by
Elaine Clayton

ALFRED A. KNOPF
NEW YORK

Text copyright © 2009 by Jane Smiley
Illustrations copyright © 2009 by Elaine Clayton

All rights reserved. Published in the United States by Alfred A. Knopf, an imprint of Random House Children's Books, a division of Random House, Inc., New York.

Knopf, Borzoi Books, and the colophon are registered trademarks of Random House, Inc.

Visit us on the Web! www.randomhouse.com/kids

Educators and librarians, for a variety of teaching tools, visit us at www.randomhouse.com/teachers

Library of Congress Cataloging-in-Publication Data
Smiley, Jane.
The Georges and the Jewels / Jane Smiley. — 1st ed.
p.   cm.
Summary: Seventh-grader Abby Lovitt grows up on her family's California horse ranch in the 1960s, learning to train the horses her father sells and trying to reconcile her strict religious upbringing with her own ideas about life.
ISBN 978-0-375-86227-4 (trade) — ISBN 978-0-375-96227-1 (lib. bdg.) — ISBN 978-0-375-89414-5 (e-book)
[1. Horses—Training—Fiction. 2. Ranch life—California—Fiction. 3. Family life—California—Fiction. 4. Christian life—Fiction. 5. California—History—1950—Fiction.]
I. Title.
PZ7.S6413Ge 2009
[Fic]—dc22
2009006241

The text of this book is set in 11.5-point Goudy.

Printed in the United States of America
September 2009
10 9 8 7 6 5 4 3 2 1
First Edition

The
Georges
and the
Jewels

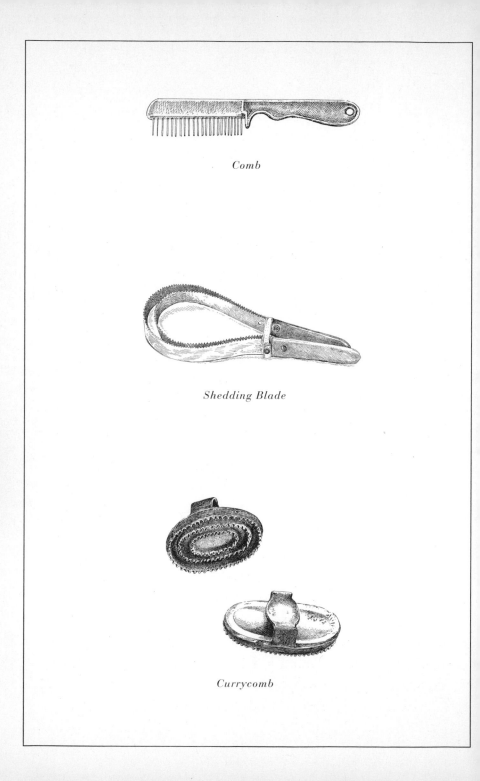

Comb

Shedding Blade

Currycomb

Chapter 1

SOMETIMES WHEN YOU FALL OFF YOUR HORSE, YOU JUST DON'T want to get right back on. Let's say he started bucking and you did all the things you knew to do, like pull his head up from between his knees and make him go forward, then use a pulley rein on the left to stop him. Most horses would settle at that point and come down to a walk. Then you could turn him again and trot off—it's always harder for the horse to buck at the trot than at the lope. But if, right when you let up on the reins, your horse put his head between his knees again and took off bucking, kicking higher and higher until he finally dropped you and went tearing off to the other end of the ring, well, you might lie there, as I did, with the wind knocked out of you and think about how nice it would be not to get back on, because that horse is just dedicated to bucking you off.

So I did lie there, looking up at the branches of the oak tree that grew beside the ring, and I did wait for Daddy to come trotting over with that horse by the bridle, and I did stare up at both their faces, the face of that horse flicking his ears back and forth and snorting a little bit, and the face of my father, red-cheeked and blue-eyed, and I did listen to him say, "Abby? You okay, honey? Sure you are. I saw you bounce! Get up, now."

I sighed.

"How am I going to tell those folks who are looking to buy these horses that a little girl can ride them, if you don't get up and ride them?"

I sat up. I said, "I don't know, Daddy." My elbow hurt, but not too badly. Otherwise I was okay.

"Well, then."

I stood up, and he brushed off the back of my jeans. Then he tossed me on the horse again.

Some horses buck you off. Some horses spook you off—they see something scary and drop a shoulder and spin and run away. Some horses stop all of a sudden, and there you are, head over heels and sitting on the ground. I had a horse rear so high once that I just slid down over her tail and landed in the grass easy as you please, watching her run back to the barn. I started riding when I was three. I started training horses for my dad when I was eight. I wasn't the only one—my brother, Danny, was thirteen at the time, and he did most of the riding (Kid's Horse for Sale), but I'm the only one now.

Which is not to say that there aren't good horses and fun horses. I ride plenty of those, too. But they don't last, because Daddy turns those over fast. I had one a year ago, a sweet bay mare. We got her because her owner had died and Daddy picked her up for a song from the bank. I rode her every day, and she never put a foot wrong. Her lope was as easy as flying. One of the days she was with us, I had a twenty-four-hour virus, so when I went out to ride, I tacked her up and took her down to the crick at the bottom of the pasture, out of sight of the house.

I knew Daddy had to go into town and would be gone for the afternoon, so when I got down there, I just took off the saddle and hung it over a tree limb, and the bridle, too, and I lay down in the grass and fell asleep. I knew she would graze, and she did for a while, I suppose. But when I woke up (and feeling much better, thank you), there she was, curled up next to me like a dog, kind of pressed against me but sweet and large and soft. I lay there feeling how warm she was and smelling her fragrance, and I thought, I never heard of this before. I don't know why she did that, but now when Daddy tells me that horses only know two things, the carrot and the stick, and not to fill my head with silly ideas about them, I just remember that mare (she had a star shaped like a triangle and a little snip down by her left nostril). We sold her for a nice piece of change within a month, and I wish I knew where she was.

But Daddy names all the mares Jewel and all the geldings George, and I can hardly remember which was which after a while.

The particular George who bucked me off had a hard mouth. I did the best I could with him for another twenty minutes, but Daddy said that probably he was going to have to get on him himself, which meant that we weren't going to turn this one over fast, because a little girl couldn't ride him yet. Which meant that Daddy was in a bad mood for the rest of the day.

We took the George back up to the barn, and while Daddy threw out the hay, I brushed the George off. He didn't mind, but he didn't love it like some of them do. Then I picked out his feet and took him out and put him into one of the big corrals. We didn't keep horses in stalls unless we had to, because Daddy said that they did better outside anyway, and if you kept them in stalls, well, then, you spent your life cleaning stalls rather than riding. Was that what I wanted?

I always said, "No, Daddy," and he ruffled my hair.

In the winter, though, it bothered me to think of them huddled out in the rain, their tails into the wind and their heads down. Of course that was what horses were meant to do, and ours had heavy coats, but I would lie awake when it rained in the night, wishing for it to stop.

It was worse in Oklahoma.

Oklahoma was where we came from, where Daddy and Mom grew up and had Danny, then me. We moved to California in 1957, when I was four and a half. I could barely remember living there, though we went back once or twice a year to see my grandparents and buy some horses. In Oklahoma, there could be real rain, and real snow, and real ice. Daddy had seen a horse slide right down a hill once, just couldn't stop himself, went down like he was on skis and right over the edge of a crick, fell on the ice, and had to be pulled out with a tractor. Couldn't be saved. At least in California we didn't have ice.

It was only five when we got into the house, not even suppertime, but it was January and the days were short. Christmas was over and school would start again on Monday, which meant I could ride two horses in the afternoon at most. Now that my shoulder and my arm were starting to hurt from my fall, I didn't

4

mind a break from the riding. It was just that I was sorry to be going back to school. Seventh grade. I've never heard anyone who had a single nice thing to say about seventh grade.

The next day was church. We went to church twice on Sundays—from nine to twelve in the morning and from two to four in the afternoon—and also Wednesday evening. Daddy was an elder in the church, and the place we had found, that we called our chapel, was really just a big room in a strip mall, with a cleaners on one side and a Longs drugstore on the other. Daddy and Mr. Hazen were looking for another place, maybe a church that was for sale (you'd be surprised at how many churches get sold when the congregation decides it needs more room), but they hadn't found one yet, so between noon and two, we kids wandered around that strip mall and went into Longs and looked at the comic books (until we got caught) or the toys or the makeup or the medical supplies, whatever there was that might be interesting. Sometimes Daddy drove me home to check on the horses, and sometimes he went by himself. Mom always offered, but Daddy said she had enough to do, setting up the lunch for the brothers and sisters.

The brothers and sisters were mostly fairly old—older than Daddy and Mom. Only three families had kids, us and the Hollingsworths and the Greeleys. We had me, the Hollingsworths had Carlie, Erica, and Bobby, who were all younger than Danny and older than I. The Greeley kids were four, two, and one. Sometimes, on a really unlucky day, Carlie Hollingsworth and I would be told to watch the Greeleys, and then our hands were full, because those Greeleys, even the baby, could run. What Mom said, if I made a face, was "Sally and Sam need a break, so you can do your share."

The only thing I liked about church, though I didn't say this to Daddy or Mom, was the singing. To tell the truth, I never knew what songs were really hymns, because Daddy, Mom, Mrs. Greeley, and Mr. Hazen were ready to sing anything, and some Sundays we would sing for an hour at a time, more like a songfest than a church service. On those days, Daddy always came home happy. We sang "Farther Along" and "When the Roll Is Called Up Yonder, I'll Be There," "Abide with Me," and "Amazing Grace." We didn't have hymnals—Daddy said we might get those next year—but someone always knew the words anyway and would teach the others. It wasn't right that the singing would push into the preaching of the Gospel, but sometimes it did and I didn't mind. On the days when there was more preaching and less singing, Daddy came home in a worse mood.

That Sunday after I fell off, I was still a little stiff, so rather than wander around Longs, I stayed with Mom and helped her serve the food. She had macaroni and cheese, baked beans, some broccoli and carrots, a loaf of bread, and a wedge of cheese. For dessert, Mrs. Greeley had made an applesauce cake, which I liked very much. The younger women always made a lot of food, because, Mom said, for some of the old people, this was the biggest meal they got all week. "You know you are going home to a nice supper, Abby, so you watch what you eat, because Mrs. Larkin doesn't have that, and neither does Mrs. Lodge." I watched what I ate, but I especially watched myself eat a piece of that applesauce cake.

The second service was more like Sunday school. The grown-ups went to one side of the room and studied the Bible, and the kids went to another side of the room and did things like read Bible stories and color Bible coloring books. There was also a felt board that Mrs. Larkin sometimes brought, on which she did felt shows. There would be a cutout of Joseph, say, made of white felt, and then a bunch of cutouts of his brothers, and some felt palm trees that represented Egypt and a felt house that represented Israel, and she moved the felt pieces around on the board while telling us the story. I think she had pieces for six or eight different stories. For the most part, everyone at church was nice.

This was not true of seventh grade. Monday morning, I got on the bus. Because we had horses to feed and water before school, I was always the last person on the bus, and fairly often the driver had to stop after he had already started and open the door again for me. The impossible thing was deciding whether to get dressed first and then do the work or to get dressed, do the work, and change again before going to school. If I slept in, even a little, I could not get dressed twice, and so my shoes would be a little dirty when I got on the bus. Sometimes the other kids started yelling, "Hey! What's that smell? Hey, what smells so bad in here?" and sometimes they didn't, but I always expected them to. I didn't have any friends on the bus, so I tried to read a book or look out the window.

The best thing that can happen to you in seventh grade, really, is that you float from one classroom to another like a ghost or a spirit, undetected by the humans. I thought maybe it would be possible to do that at one of those big schools in a big town, but our school was small, the seventh grade had forty kids divided into two classes, and everyone had a slot. My home-room teacher was Mr. Jepsen, the math teacher. It did not help that numbers made my head hurt. If I could sit by myself at night and work out my homework problems, I almost always got them all right, but Mr. Jepsen was the kind of teacher who likes to interrupt. "So, Abby, what's the square root of sixty-four?" and then, just when you are opening your mouth to say, "Eight," he says, "Cat got your tongue today? Are you thinking?" And then when you open your mouth again, he says, "Well, what's the square root of sixteen?" and now you're in this rhythm—every time you have the answer, he asks you another question, until he gives up on you and finally says, "Billy Russell?" and of course, Billy Russell has been sitting there for five minutes, thinking about the answer, and he pipes up, "Eight!" as bright as he can be, and Mr. Jepsen says, "Good boy!"

Or, if you happened to look out the window, as soon as your eyes went in that direction, Mr. Jepsen would say, "Abby, is the great outdoors that much more fascinating than this classroom?" and of course you couldn't say yes, you had to keep your mouth shut. Most of the other kids seemed to like Mr. Jepsen, at least they laughed at all of his jokes. Even so, I had a B in math—A on homework and tests, C on class participation—and that was good enough for Daddy, who didn't expect me to be going to college anyway.

In our seventh grade, there were only thirteen girls. Eight of them were in the other section. The four girls I liked least—the Big Four was what they had called themselves since fifth grade—were all in my section, and Gloria, who had been my friend since kindergarten, was in the other section and I didn't see her much. All day I wondered if, at the end of the day, she would still be my friend or whether those seven girls in the other section would finally capture her. We had one new girl this year, Stella Kerkhoff, who had come into seventh grade from another school in the district. She had tried to be friends with almost everyone in the class and discovered what we all knew—that there was no room in the Big Four for a fifth wheel, that Maria, Fatima, and Lucia kept to themselves, that Debbie Perkins (who I was friends with in third and fourth grade) was not only amazingly quiet, but also lived on a ranch at the furthest end of the school district and could never come over or have guests, and that the Goldman twins, even though they were friendly, really were twins—it was hard to tell them apart (and they didn't mind playing tricks about that), they didn't really need another friend, and anyway, they were so smart they took half their classes with the eighth graders.

So Stella had decided before Christmas that Gloria was the one—Gloria's backpack was always filled with folded-up little notes from Stella, and at lunch Stella made it her business to sit between Gloria and me whenever I didn't get there first. For the month between Thanksgiving and Christmas, I did what Mom told me and pretended not to know what was going on. Gloria did, too, so it was impossible to tell who was winning. That Monday, I was so stiff from my fall (you're always more stiff the second day than the first) that of course Stella got in there, no problem. And then they went to the girls' room together, and I was just sitting there until the bell for sixth period rang. So, it was a bad day.

And then the bus broke down on the way home and was stuck for an hour while it was getting darker and darker, and so I knew we weren't going to get any training in, and Daddy was going to say, "Well, the hay was wasted today, since the horses don't know a single thing that they didn't know yesterday."

All of this is just a prologue to the thing that happened next.

Bridle Without Reins

Braided Rope Reins

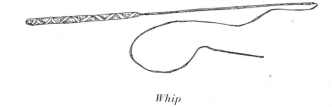

Whip

Chapter 2

THE NEXT MORNING, TUESDAY, OF COURSE, I HAD MADE UP MY mind not to get caught by the school bus, so I got up really early. It was dark and pretty cold. Even by the time I was dressed and ready to go out and start with the hay, Daddy and Mom were still in bed. I didn't mind that—I did the morning work by myself fairly often, and I liked hearing the horses nicker to me, seeing them standing by the gate looking for something to eat. Even horses who don't know you or don't like you are happy to see you if you have an armload of alfalfa.

I hayed the Georges first, the littler George (chestnut), the George who had dumped me (named, as far as I was concerned, Ornery George), and the pony George. Then I went back in the barn and came out with hay for the Jewels. We only had two mares at the time—Daddy had just sold two to a ranch up in the valley, nice horses and pretty enough so that he could get a little extra for them. He always said, "Even the most dried-up old cowboy will pay for a good-looker, and don't you let them tell you different. You could have the greatest horse in the world, and if it had a head like a bathtub, I couldn't sell it for beans."

But only one of the Jewels was standing by the gate. That was a bad sign, and I was glad that it was starting to get light in case there was something out there in the paddock that I had to look for and report back. I threw down the hay in three piles, the way you're supposed to, one more than the number of horses so they won't fight over it, and then I climbed the gate. Most of the mares' pasture wasn't visible from the gate—it ran in a gentle slope down to the crick. For a while I didn't see anything. Then, over to one side, I saw the second mare, standing under a tree. She turned her head toward me. She wasn't down and she didn't look like she was in trouble. When I got a little closer, I saw that she had something with her, and then, when I got closer than that, I saw that that something was a foal. The foal was standing next to the mare, and when it saw me, it skittered around to the other side of her and peeked at me under the mare's neck. When I got even closer, I could just see its legs and its nose.

You never know with a mare, no matter how friendly she is on her own, how she will react to you when she has a foal at her side, so I stopped and stood there. After a minute or two, the foal came around the mare again, gave me a look, and then began to nurse, his back end to me and his little tail switching back and forth. He looked to me to be at least six or eight hours old, which meant that maybe he was born before we went to bed and we just missed the mare in the dark. When you don't know a mare is pregnant, I guess it never occurs to you to wonder whether she is having a foal.

This Jewel was one of three horses Daddy had bought right after Thanksgiving. One he had sold already, and the ornery George was the third one. What with Christmas and all, we hadn't done a lot with her or even paid much attention to her, though I thought she was nice, and I always gave her a few extra pats. She was pretty without being distinctive—no white on her at all, not too big, not too small, good head, decent feet.

Now it was getting to be day. I took one step toward the mare, watching her, and then another and another. She looked at me, but she didn't pin her ears and start switching her tail, and so I took another step. The foal kept nursing, his tail turned to me. He didn't have any white stockings that I could see. I took another step. The foal's head popped up and he ran around the mare again, so that she was between the foal and me. Now I was fairly close, close enough to lean forward, stretch out my hand, and touch the mare on the neck. I watched her, though, before I tried. She still gave no warning signs, so I stretched out my hand, leaned forward from my hips, and touched her, then I touched her again, just a little stroke, down her neck. I took one step closer. Then I was very still. The mare's tail moved slowly back and forth, and the face of the foal appeared. Its little dark ears were pricked and its nostrils wide, and it was staring at me. No white on the face. Prominent forehead. "Hey, baby," I said softly.

And now there was a shout from up the hill—"Abby! AAABBYYY!" Daddy's voice. "Ruth Abigail! You out there?" He only calls me by my full name when he's worried or mad.

I was backing slowly away from the mare and foal, not wanting to shout and startle them.

Daddy appeared on the brow of the hill. I could see him out of the corner of my eye. Surely from there he could take it all in—me, mare, foal. I backed up two more steps. There was a silence. Then I heard him say, "What the—" He never finished this sentence, because he never spoke the name of the Lord in an idle fashion, but sometimes he came close.

I turned and ran up the hill.

He said, "Is that a foal?"

"It is, Daddy. It's so big and pretty."

We stood there for a minute, and Daddy said, "Well, I'll be—" And then, "It's always one trial or another."

"Should we bring them in?"

"And put her where? Those stalls aren't clean enough for a foal. They're better off out here."

"But it's cold."

"Well, she should have thought of that before foaling out, don't you think?"

I looked at him. We were walking up the hill, almost to the gate by now.

"Mares can wait, you know, not like humans. You ask your mom about it. I've heard of mares going three hundred eighty days, just because the weather's no good." With every word he said, I sensed him getting less and less happy.

I said, "It's so cute, Daddy. It doesn't have a speck of white on it. It's got a pretty head."

"What can I do with a foal? What can I do with a mare who has a foal? Can't wean it for five months, then it'll take another two months or so to get her in shape. That's seven months of burning hay before we can even begin to sell her. That's probably why they sold her to us in the first place—they knew she was in foal and they didn't want to deal with it. Woke up one morning and one of the stallions was out with the mares, or something like that, so they crossed their fingers behind their back and threw her in with the others just to get rid of her."

Mom was at the door. "What? What is it? Is everyone okay?"

"Got a foal is all," said Daddy as he went past her into the kitchen.

"A foal!" She put her hands on my shoulders. "Do they look okay?"

I said, "It looks great, Mom!"

"Should we call the vet?"

Daddy said, "First, we'll call the Lord. The Lord will decide."

I kind of did not like that, because in my experience, the Lord didn't always decide as I would have.

Daddy said, "Abby can help me outside. She's already missed the school bus."

Mom looked at the clock and said, "Well, she has."

That was the second good thing to happen that day, and it was only seven a.m.

We had some toast and went back out. The first thing we had to do was clean the biggest stall and put all new straw in, and lots of it. I was happy to think that the Jewel and her foal would be able to snuggle down into the bedding and stay warm. Then we took a halter down to where the mare was. We approached her carefully, but she was friendly, just the way she had been before she foaled. After I put the halter on her, Daddy stood looking at the baby. It was now full day, and even I could see that he was a colt, and a nice one—strong, with a well-set neck and an alert look about him. He wasn't crowding against the mare, either—he already had a mind of his own ("Not a good sign," said Daddy).

The colt would turn away from the mare and stare out over the crick or up the hill, then leap into the air and kick out or trot around in a little circle, and she would nicker at him, but not sounding as though she was worried. More of an "I'm here" than a "Watch out!" In the end, we didn't try to touch him, we just walked the mare slowly up the hill, letting her stop and call him anytime she wanted to. He came along, but not without jumping and frolicking. I couldn't stand the idea that we might name him George, but Daddy was strict about the names because he said I already got too attached to some of them. If he let me name them, then I would pine for them after they were gone. So I didn't say anything.

When we got to the top of the hill, Daddy held the other mare so that she wouldn't try anything, and we went through the gate. The Georges were all eyes and ears, too. Every one of the horses was whinnying.

The hardest thing was getting the colt into the stall. The way we did that was, I held open the stall door as wide as it would go, Mom stood inside with Jewel, and Daddy ranged around behind the foal, not driving it, but being a barrier if it wanted to go away. The key was to let the mare call him and let him find her. Even though it took a few minutes for him to make up his mind to go through that scary doorway, and even though her nickers got just a little louder and more nervous, neither one did panic, and pretty soon we had them locked in the stall. If you ask me, the mare looked relieved. She had a nice clean bucket of water and she drank about half of it. The colt gave us a stare and then started to nurse.

Mom said, "Did you look around down there?"

Daddy shook his head, then said, "You two should do that. It's time she learned."

"What?" I asked.

Mom said, "We've got to go down the hill and look around for the bag and placenta. We've got to see if all the placenta came out."

"I guess you'll tell me what that is when we get there."

"You know what that is. It's what feeds the baby through the umbilical cord when it's inside the mother. If any of it stays inside the mare, she can die."

"Let's go!"

But the placenta was there, lying crumpled in the grass. Mom carefully laid it out, fitting together the pieces we could find the way you would a jigsaw puzzle. "Seems complete," she said. "We had a mare once—" But then she decided not to tell me that story, and so I knew it was a bad one.

"Daddy doesn't like the foal."

"A foal is a lot of work. And a colt is more work. A big lively colt is the most work."

When we got back up the hill, Daddy said, "Well, I guess if you aren't going to school today, you'd better start riding."

I rode the pony George first. Daddy said that there usually wasn't much market for a pony, but when someone needed one, then a pony was exactly what they needed and the only thing. Our pony was medium-sized—he came up about to my chin (all the horses were taller than I was by at least an inch or two). Once the spring rolled around, Daddy thought he could sell that pony to some people who had an English riding school out on the coast. In the meantime, no pony burned much hay—in fact, you had to be really careful about giving a pony too much feed or it would founder, which is when a horse's feet get hot and swell inside the wall of the hoof, except there's nowhere for the feet to swell to but down through the sole, so the horse (or pony) can get crippled and die.

I rode the pony around the ring with the English saddle, walk, trot, canter, turn right, turn left, back up, go in a big circle, go in a little circle. Three days a week of this was enough for the pony. Once I had untacked him and picked his feet and put him back with the other Georges, I went and peeked in the stall.

The foal was lying down, his back legs folded underneath him and his front legs stretched out. He had his nose on his knees and his eyes closed, but then he lifted his head and looked at me, his ears flicking back and forth. The mare nickered to him, a low ruffling sound, and he put his nose up to her. She touched it with her own, then took another bite of her hay. Behind me, Mom said, "Now, it's okay to look at them, but you let him and her get to know each other for three or four days before you introduce yourself. Sometimes if you get between a mare and a foal and get your smell on the foal, she'll reject him." The foal flopped over and stretched out in the straw. His legs looked incredibly long and thin, loose, like noodles. If I hadn't seem him jump around on them, I wouldn't have thought such a thing was possible.

After the pony, I rode the other Jewel, then the chestnut George. They were little girl material all the way. Then Daddy said, "Okay, Abby, get up on that one again." He tossed his head toward Ornery George.

"I thought you were going to ride him a couple of times."

"My back hurts. My feet hurt."

"I don't believe you."

"I think you'll do fine. I don't want him to get used to me. Sometimes when a strong man pushes a horse around and makes him do what he's supposed to, then he's worse when the girl gets back on him. You rode him fine before. Let's just try it."

I knew better than to say I didn't want to try it.

But in spite of how nice the pony had been and the other two horses, it made me nervous to put my foot in the stirrup, and then when he stepped away from me and pinned his ears, I felt my mouth get dry. That was a new one for me. Daddy came up behind me and threw me into the saddle and said, "Now go forward. Don't give him a chance to think about it."

I kicked his sides and he squirted forward, then went off at a trot. I tried to remember what my goal was—Daddy said I was to have a goal every time I got on. After thinking hard about my goal for a few seconds, I decided that it was only to be less nervous. I took some deep breaths.

"What are you all stiffening up for? You look like you're riding a pogo stick."

19

I made my hips loosen up and I straightened the small of my back so that I sat more deeply in the saddle. He said, "That's better."

When we got to the end of the ring, we trotted back, then did a few circles in both directions. George seemed half asleep. Daddy said, "Stir him up. He's ignoring you."

I slapped his sides with my legs, and there he was, kicking out. He kicked out so high that he nearly tossed me over the front. As it was, I got the saddle horn in my stomach. He stopped, I kicked him on, he kicked up again, I pulled him up.

"Now he's got you," said Daddy. "He's got your number and he's dialing it. He's saying, 'Abby, I don't want to go and you can't make me.'"

"I can't."

"You can."

"I can't."

"You have to. *You* have to. It doesn't matter if I do. It's your number he's got, not mine."

While we were talking, he'd come over to me, and now he was standing, looking up at me, his hand on the pommel of the saddle. I could feel that I was shaking now, both because Daddy was giving me his sternest look and because I could feel George beneath me, ready to take off again. I took some more deep breaths and said, "I can't." Then I said something I hadn't ever said before: "And I'm not going to."

Daddy wasn't always as strict about sassing as he thought he was—you could say, "I would rather not," or, "No, thanks," and sometimes he would give in. But I had used "a tone" with him, so now I looked down, so as not to have him stare at me anymore, and jumped off. I handed him the reins, then walked away, back toward the barn, where I couldn't resist peeking at the colt. But then I went out the other end of the barn and around into the house without letting Daddy see me. I went up to my room and closed the door. There was always homework.

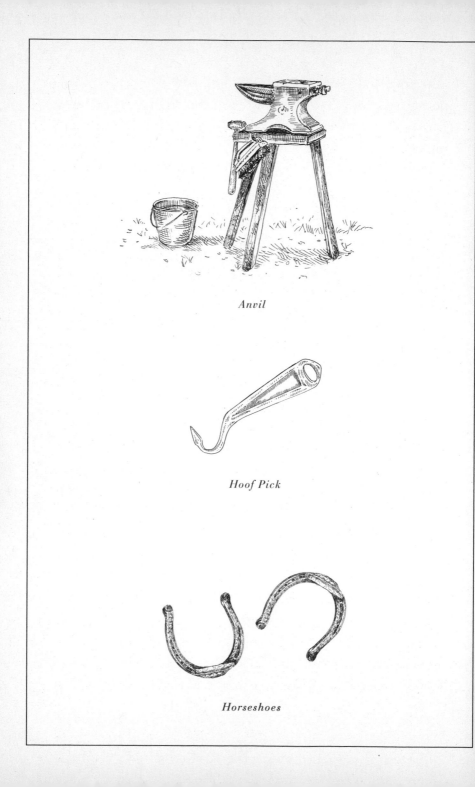

Anvil

Hoof Pick

Horseshoes

Chapter 3

MY BROTHER, DANNY, DIDN'T GET KICKED OUT FOR TALKING back to Daddy, but that's how it started. We call him Danny, Mom and I, but Daddy has always called him Daniel, because that was the real biblical name. Daddy wanted Danny to grow into his name—Daniel. There was a time when I was a little kid when Daddy and Daniel were "just like this!" as Mom would say, putting her forefinger and her middle finger together and holding them up for you to see. But after Danny turned twelve and got to be as tall as Daddy, they went from being "just like this" to being "cut from the same cloth," and it was a rough, tough cloth. Neither one of them could say anything that the other didn't disagree with, which meant that Daddy considered Danny "ornery" and Danny considered Daddy "stubborn." It didn't help that they looked pretty much alike and could stare each other down, eye to eye. The whole thing made my mom very sad, but there wasn't a thing she could do about it. She would say, "It's hard to be a man in the Lovitt family," and then shake her head.

I remember on the day Daddy kicked Danny out, which was before Halloween, I was in my room with the door open, braiding a set of reins. I heard Mom go into Danny's room and start in with him. She said, "Honey, it's fine for you to read any book you want, especially if it's a schoolbook, but you don't have to discuss it with him or even tell him what's in it. You know it will make him mad, so just keep it to yourself."

"He should know about evolution."

"He does know about that."

"Then why didn't he ever tell me? So that when I raise my hand in science class and make my contribution, as Mr. Freer wants me to do, they can all laugh at me? It's a good thing I'm bigger than all those guys, or I would have gotten beat up over lunch period."

"Well, your dad and the science teacher disagree about a few things, but you can learn what the science teacher has to teach you and read the book and make up your own mind without getting into it with your dad."

"I can?"

"You can. I wish you would."

Danny generally did what Mom told him, so what happened at the table wasn't precisely about the science class thing. However, it was about breaking rules. It was Saturday-night supper. Because Mom had to cook for church the next day, we were having something simple—just some minute steaks and gravy with rice and string beans. It was good. Then Danny said, "I'm going to the movies with Frankie Horner. He drives and he's picking me up. I've got the money myself."

"You're not going out with a pack of boys alone in a car."

"It's not a pack of boys. It's me and Frankie and one other guy. We're going to a movie."

"What movie?"

"It's just *Frankenstein Meets the Space Monster*. It's—"

"It's a piece of foolishness, I'm sure."

"Well, yeah, but the other kids said it was good. It's been out for weeks. Everybody's seen it—"

"And if every kid in your class—"

Mom and I gave each other a look.

"Poked a rattler with a sharp stick—"

Danny started scowling and then said in his own sarcastic voice, "Would you get in line to poke it, too?"

Daddy slammed down his knife and fork. Danny had never talked quite like that before. Mom said, "Danny—"

I said, "Daddy—"

And then Danny said, "Goddammit." And he said it in a voice that you would only use if you had said it before, more than once, and if you were used to saying it, not as if it was the first time.

Daddy said, in his extra-quiet, you-better-watch-it tone, "What was that?"

I don't know that Danny had realized what he was saying

before he said it, and maybe he was sorry, but it was clear as day that he wasn't going to back down, and then he said, "I said, 'Goddammit.' What I meant was, 'Goddammit to hell.'"

"So," said Daddy, "some boys who taught you to take the holy name of the Lord in vain are going to pick you up and take you to see a fantasy movie about evil and hate. Am I right?"

Danny backed down a little here, and he said, "It's harmless. I'm s—"

But now Daddy was madder, because the way it works with him, something starts him off, and at first he's not so mad, but then he thinks about it a little and he gets hotter and hotter. Usually he has to go in his room and pray and seek the righteousness of the Lord before he calms down (though Mom said it was worse before I was born). Anyway, Daddy didn't hear Danny begin to back off, and so he leaned forward across the table and landed a blow, the chastisement of the Lord, which was a punch across the jaw. This knocked Danny out of his chair, but he came up swinging and crawled across the table, putting his knee in the green beans, and returned the punch, and then the two of them fell off the table and were rolling around on the floor, yelling and hitting. And truly, I had never seen anything like this in my life. My mother jumped up and was shouting, "Mark! Daniel! Mark! Daniel!" but they didn't pay one bit of attention to her.

Finally, Daddy had Danny pinned because after all, he did outweigh him quite a bit, and by this time Danny was crying. Daddy let him up, saying, "Dear Lord forgive me!" but Danny wasn't going to forgive him, and he went into his room and packed a bag, and when those boys arrived in their car, even though Daddy was shouting, "Don't you go with them, young man! Don't you do it or you will find yourself in very hot water!" Danny walked out the door with his bag and never looked back.

He came home a couple of days later for more stuff, and he and Daddy haven't spoken since, though Mom goes and sees Danny from time to time and takes him things like biscuits and bread and probably money, though he doesn't need money, because he works for the horseshoer, Jake Morrisson, and even though Jake shoes our horses and Danny doesn't come over when Jake does, Daddy doesn't mind that he has a real job and a hard job.

One night, I heard him say to Mom, "It's just as well that he doesn't go to school anymore, because the higher you get in school, the more they teach you that's against the Lord." But they won't speak until Danny is moved to come forth with a humble and sincere apology and reaffirm the authority of his father, which I don't think is going to happen. Daddy and Mom pretend that everything is fine. Daddy even said once that he himself left home at sixteen and started supporting himself, and what's wrong with that?

What's wrong with it was that everyone was so angry and that Danny didn't help me ride the horses anymore. Daddy pretended that everything was the same as it was the previous year when we had ten horses waiting to be sold and they were getting ridden every day and really working. Ten horses in the late winter was good. Along about March, just when you'd gotten them ready, spring came, the flowers bloomed, and the buyers started feeling like they needed new mounts, or better mounts, or prettier mounts. Daddy could make enough in March to be a nice cushion for the whole rest of the year. This year we had five horses, and now it was four, until the foal was weaned.

These were not the things I was thinking about when I refused to ride Ornery George, but I thought about them later, that night in my bed. Danny and Daddy had been "cut from the same cloth" for so long that our house was quieter and more peaceful without him, and sometimes I was glad of that, or at least relieved. But Danny had always been fun for me— never (well, hardly ever) the kind of brother who hits or teases, more the kind of brother who teaches you to play checkers and pick-up sticks, or helps you saddle your horse, or lets you have the last cookie if you really want it. I missed him, but it was hard to get to see him, so I tried not to think about it. Daddy said that it was the job of the prodigal to return, not the job of the righteous to go after him.

The next day, of course, I had school again. I sat through math (unilateral equations), science (the cell), English (*Hard Times*), social studies (the Pharaohs), health (protein, fats, and carbohydrates), and homeroom. Through all of these classes, the Big Four (Linda, Mary A., Mary N., and Joan) sat in a single row in the front, passing notes when Mr. Jepsen wasn't looking and poring over their books when he was. They weren't actively mean to me, but I had known since fifth grade that they would be if they thought I was acting "weird" or "stupid," so I sat across the aisle from them, beside the window, not looking out, but thinking of the foal. Already, after only a single day, he was stronger and more inquisitive. When I went out to feed that morning, he had been peering over the top of the stall door, just to see what he could see, and though I didn't touch him, he looked as though he would have let me if I'd tried. His eyes said, "Who are you? What do you want?" I just murmured in a low voice, "You'll see, little buddy, you will certainly see."

Stella and Gloria sat with me at lunch, no problem. Stella was extra nice to me. "Oh, Abby. I know you like oranges, and I don't care. Here's mine. I'll eat your apple." While I was sharing the orange with Gloria, Stella leaned toward us and said, "He called me again last night. We talked for half an hour." She glanced over her shoulder at Brian Connelly. Brian Connelly was a boy Gloria and I had known since kindergarten, who had spent the first four years of elementary school picking his nose. He was now kind of good-looking. His mom let him grow his hair long, for one thing, and he also liked to talk to girls, which was a rarity among the boys we knew.

She whispered, as if it were a secret, "He says he got a stereo of his own for Christmas! So did I! We both thought that was such a coincidence. And I got a Dusty Springfield album and he got a Rolling Stones album. And you know, Dusty Springfield and the Rolling Stones are *both* English, so we thought that was a coincidence. He doesn't like the Beach Boys at all."

Gloria rolled her eyes, but discreetly, as if she were sort of laughing at Stella, but not really. At my house, at any rate, we didn't listen to the Rolling Stones or Dusty Springfield or the

Beach Boys. More Bob Wills and Porter Wagoner on the radio or on Mom's old record player that only played 45s. Danny probably listened to all of those English bands now, but I didn't know. Even so, I said, "My brother likes Dusty Springfield."

"She's really pretty," said Stella.

"Yeah," I said.

Gloria made a face.

Stella went on, "I love the way she does her makeup."

"Let's talk about something else," said Gloria.

I said, "We had a foal."

"What's that?" said Stella.

Gloria snorted, but I decided to be nice. I said, "It's a baby horse."

"I thought that was a colt or something."

"It is a colt. Our foal is a colt. A colt is a male and a filly is a female, and a foal is just a baby."

"Is it cute?"

"Really—" But the foal wasn't cute, I thought, he was . . . stirring. I said, "I don't know if—"

"You know what Brian told me?"

"What?" said Gloria.

"He said that Martin Selden likes you."

"Who, me?" said Gloria.

Stella nodded excitedly.

"I think I'm going to puke," said Gloria.

I said, "Right now?"

"If I have to."

"But—" said Stella.

Gloria turned her back on Stella and leaned toward me. She said, "Can I come home with you on the bus and see the foal? My mom wouldn't mind. She'd like to see it when she picks me up. I can call her from your house."

Over Gloria's shoulder, I could see Stella looking a little surprised. I didn't know what I thought about that. I would have expected to be happy, but I wasn't, really. Gloria could be pretty mean if she lost patience. I said, "Not today. Not till he's three or four days old, my daddy says."

Gloria flipped her hair over her shoulder, practically in Stella's face, and said, "Okay, we'll come over the weekend, then. That will be fun." She didn't say a word about Stella coming along, and neither did I, since it was Gloria's idea. But when the bell rang, and they went to their sixth period, they were laughing.

That afternoon, I rode the pony, the chestnut George, and the Jewel. All three were extra good, and Daddy even dragged out some poles and tubs and had me jump the pony over some cross-poles. Every time the pony jumped, Daddy laughed and said, "Look at those knees! Right together and up around his chin." Then he went inside and got a tablecloth. To tell the truth, it was the very one that we were eating off of that week, but Mom must have been somewhere else. Anyway, Daddy set a pole so that it was straight across two of the smaller tubs and draped that tablecloth over the pole so it fluttered a little in the wind. He said, "Now take him over that."

I was sitting on the pony about twenty paces from the jump, just beginning to wonder whether I liked that idea, when the pony picked up a trot and trotted right down toward the fluttering cloth. I sat tight, not knowing what he would do, but I didn't kick him or turn him off. I just looked over the top of the jump at the peak of the barn roof, and sure enough, he picked up a canter and popped over that square of fabric like he'd done it a hundred times. Daddy said, "I bet this little guy'd jump anything, really."

I knew what that meant.

Now Daddy got a bee in his bonnet. For the next few days, he went looking for anything you could possibly jump. Not only the tablecloth, but a couple of kitchen chairs, a row of wastebaskets, the wheelbarrow, a low clothesline hung with dish towels, a length of picket fence, two hay bales with a place setting of dishes on them. The pony jumped everything. Daddy got happier and happier and said that in the spring, he would take me to the coast, where they had the English-style horse shows, because that pony was like gold coins in the bank, and he was pretty, too, gray with black points and a black mane. Every day I was to brush him all over and then rub him with a folded-up piece of an old woolen sweater to make him shine.

The pony didn't seem to mind the foal, so after I rode, when I was doing the extra grooming, I cross-tied him in the aisle outside the stall where the mare and foal lived. The foal would stand there, looking at us and flicking his ears back and forth and ruffling his nostrils. He had a high whinny that made me laugh, and sometimes he just whinnied all at once for no reason, even though his mom was standing right behind him, eating her hay. Then the foal would give a high squeal and lift up on his hind legs for a moment and toss his head like he had more energy than he knew what to do with. But I still didn't go up to him or pet him, even though it seemed to me that he was saying, with every look and every whinny, "Come here! Come here! I want to get to know you!"

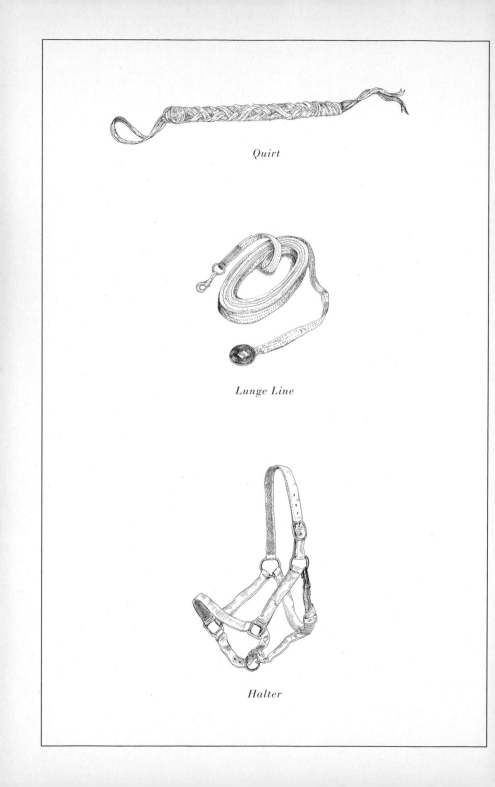

Quirt

Lunge Line

Halter

Chapter 4

ON SATURDAY MORNING, THE FOAL WAS FIVE DAYS OLD. IT WAS a nice day—not wet and almost warm—so after breakfast, we went out to the barn, all three of us. Mom got a halter and lead rope and took the other Jewel out of the big mare corral and led her into one of the stalls. Then she put the halter on the foal's dam, opened the stall door, and brought her out. Daddy and I stood to either side of the door, ready to guide the foal if he went the wrong way. Mom stopped with the mare about ten feet out into the yard, and we waited for what seemed like a long time. The foal stood in the doorway with his nose poked into the sunlight, snorting. A couple of times, he struck out with his front hooves, as if he were a big tough guy, and then he jumped through the doorway, jumped up to the mare, and pressed himself against her for a moment before Mom led her on to the corral. The mare went quietly. The foal leapt and bucked in the breeze. His ears flicked back and forth. After we closed up behind him and then shut the gate to the corral, he reared straight up into the air and galloped for about ten strides. I guess he just couldn't believe how free he was. The mare trotted after him, nickering.

Even though I had horses to ride, I stood by the fence, watching him play and laughing. Finally, I heard Daddy say, "Abby! I'm talking to you! If your friend is coming over, you'd better get started."

I turned to him. "I don't want to name him George."

"'Little George' is fine. We'd know him perfectly well by that."

"No, Daddy. He's not a George. He's too bright and—"

"Cocky?"

This was a dangerous word. Daddy hated a "cocky" horse, but I said, "Well, yeah."

Daddy sighed, took out his handkerchief, wiped his nose. Then he said, "Okay, child, I see the handwriting on the wall."

The handwriting on the wall was something in the Bible. It said, *"Mene, mene, tekel, upharsin,"* and I didn't know what it meant really. In our family it meant "Watch out, you're in trouble." But Daddy put his handkerchief back in his pocket and said, "If we've got him, we'd better do a good job with him. So name him what you like."

The colt skittered around the mare, his feet fluttering. He stopped dead and stared at us, leapt up again as if we were just too much, and then settled down and began to nurse. We both laughed. I said, "Jack is okay. Jack is better than George."

"As in Jack Sprat could eat no fat, his wife could eat no lean?"

"No, as in Jack be nimble, Jack be quick, Jack jump over the candlestick."

"Okay, but let's go for Little Jack Horner, who said, 'What a good boy am I.'" Daddy ruffled my hair, and I gave him a hug.

The pony had been jumped a lot, so we gave him the day off. The chestnut George had a long work—walk, jog, lope, a few sliding stops, some spins, and some gallops around the barrels, though not at top speed. It was fun. I worked on his manners—sidestepping to the gate so I could open it, going through, sidestepping the gate closed and waiting until I was ready to go. He was supposed to wait quietly, no shuffling his feet or trying to put his head down, and he did. He was ready to sell, really. He was just waiting for a buyer, and truly, a little girl could ride him. After I got off him, Daddy took him over to the washstand and combed out his mane and tail, which were long and full, then he trimmed his whiskers and the hair in his ears. You could just see him in a parade down Main Street, his tail flowing behind him.

In the meantime, I got on the other mare. At first, she kept taking me to the end of the ring nearest the corral where the foal was. She would stop and prick her ears. She had that stiffness in her body that sometimes means a horse is going to pull away and run off, but she didn't. She got used to the foal, and pretty soon, she was passing that end of the ring without a look in the foal's direction, though if he squealed or whinnied, she would flick her ears. She had her normal work. She wasn't as far along as the chestnut George, but she was willing enough most of the time. When I kicked her or flicked the quirt at her,

her usual response was "Do I have to, well, okay," which is fine for a riding horse. That means more people who don't really know what they are doing feel safe. She was already starting to shed, so when I was finished with her, Daddy and I each took currycombs and curried off the dull winter hair. Underneath, that Jewel had a regular bay coat, red enough. She had a kind eye and a very pretty head that would make her valuable.

So, we put her away in the stall and looked at each other.

Daddy hadn't made me ride Ornery George after I refused. Probably he complained about me to Mom, and she recommended patience, because look what happened with Danny, and Daddy didn't know how to back off, and I would change my mind in a few days—I knew all the arguments. Now, as we looked at each other, I was trying to decide how stubborn he was going to be, and he was trying to decide how stubborn I was going to be, and, to be honest, I myself didn't know how stubborn I was going to be, but then he said, "Let's put him on the line."

This meant we would take him into the arena with his saddle and bridle on and run a long tape through the ring of his bit and then up over his head behind the ears and attach it to the ring on the other side. He would then trot or canter around Daddy and get rid of some of his extra energy. Usually, Daddy wasn't a big fan of using the line, because he thought it just made them fitter and fitter without teaching them much, so I knew he was exercising mercy—after some time on the line, Ornery George would be too tired to buck, and we might get a session in during which he didn't misbehave. Part of the problem with a misbehaving horse was that the more he misbehaved, the more he got into the habit of misbehaving, and, as Daddy often said about just about everything (but mostly about smoking, which he had once done), "Old habits die hard."

Ornery George looked okay. He was a brown horse with a smallish head, good legs, an arched neck, and a short back. He had great feet, which was why Daddy had liked him in the first place—no foot, no horse. He didn't have to be shod at all, just rasped every six weeks. But he didn't ever look at you, or if he did, it was only secretly, when you weren't looking at him. Most horses, when they came from the sale barn, didn't make eye contact for a while, but then, after days of hay and grooming and talk, they would begin looking for you and at you—not only did you have feed or a carrot, but also, what were you doing? But Ornery George didn't seem to care. The whole time I was grooming him and tacking him up, he pretended that I wasn't there.

Daddy led him into the ring and went to the big end, which was empty. He stood there with the looped line in one hand and a long whip in the other, and he flicked the whip so that Ornery George would turn and trot away, which he did. The way he trotted away showed us pretty clearly that he knew what he was supposed to do, and for one circuit, he did it. But then, as he was coming around the second time, he threw up his head and spun outward with his shoulder, taking the line through Daddy's hands, then trying to gallop to the other end of the ring. Daddy dropped the whip, set his heels, and leaned back against the line. Ornery George came to a stop and tossed his head again.

"Now, Abby," Daddy called, "this is a perfect example of

why you always wear gloves when you are working a horse on a line." He pulled Ornery George back to him and returned to the end of the ring, where he got George on a shorter length of tape and made him go around in a smaller circle, closer to the fence so that the fence could control him a little. Ornery George looked grumpy, but he went around on the line, making quite a few circuits. After a while, Daddy changed the attachment and sent him in the other direction. Then he said, "Well, he doesn't make you happy to be in his company, does he?"

"His jog is smooth. In fact, all his gaits are smooth. I like that part."

"He has his good qualities. But I admit they aren't mental ones. He's quiet now, though. You want to get on him?"

This wasn't a question.

"We'll stay at this end of the ring. Just do a few things to re-mind him what a good horse is like."

The worst thing that could happen was for a purchase to be a complete bust. It was bad for us, because it was a loss of money as well as hay. And it was bad for the horse, because if he was untrainable, he might have to go to the knackers. That was where horses were killed and turned into dog food and other things. We had only ever sent one horse to the killers, a mare that was given to Daddy as a last resort, for a dollar. She was fine for a few days, and then, after she reared up on the cross-ties and struck out at him with both front feet, Daddy took her out to the ring and put her on the line. The first thing she did was not, as Ornery George had done, trot off. That mare had backed up and then run toward him where he was standing in the center, her teeth bared and her ears pinned. When he put his arm up to protect himself, she bit him through his jacket. It was kill or be killed with her, and she went off two days later.

I didn't think Ornery George would ever be like that. But if a little girl couldn't ride him, then I didn't know what would happen to him. He was the first one Daddy bought after Danny left that a kid, namely me, had not been able to manage.

I stepped up to the horse, took the reins in my left hand, put my palm on top of his neck, and bent my knee. Daddy threw me into the saddle. Ornery George didn't do anything, but he gave me a look out of the corner of his eye—"Oh, it's you." I settled into the saddle and gave him a little nudge. He walked a step or two but then stopped. Daddy had his back turned, rolling up the line. I gave Ornery George another nudge and, when he didn't move, a little kick. Then *he* gave a kick, just a little kick out with his right foot, quick. What it said was, "I'm the boss. Watch your step." I kicked him again, and he started walking forward. By the time Daddy was watching, Ornery George was going along. Daddy said, "He looks okay today."

So, Ornery George and I had a secret. It was that he was going to do things his way, and I was going to let him, and we were going to get along more or less on that basis. This is not a good secret to have with your horse, because it gives him the upper hand. You always know that there might be something you could ask him to do that he would say no to, but you don't really know what it's going to be, and you're a little afraid of finding out. But I was too chicken to argue, either with Ornery George or with Daddy, so I kicked him into the trot and went around well enough while Daddy said, "He's not a bad horse. Good-looking, nice mover, a little on the dull side. I think I made a good deal for him. He'll work out."

Secretly, Ornery George and I said, "I guess we'll see about that."

Everything we did, we did just enough. His jog was just lively enough. His walk was just energetic enough. He took the proper lead at the lope, but I had to think about making him do it. He dropped into the halt, but not in a balanced way, more as if he weren't bothering to go forward any longer. A halt, as Daddy always said, is different than just stopping. A halt is as much of an exercise as a lope or a jump. You want the horse to think about it, set himself up, and then come to a standstill. Ornery George just stopped. A horse that just stops is doing what he wants to do, not what you want to do. He reined back. He was okay at that, though his ears flattened to show he was unhappy.

I did some figure eights at the trot, trying to make nice circles. When I tried it at the lope, dropping back to the trot to change leads, he bunched up a little for a buck or two but didn't actually do it, even though at the thought he might, my heart began to pound a little. After about twenty-five minutes, Daddy was satisfied, and I dismounted. As I led Ornery George back to the barn to be untacked and groomed, he and I continued to have our secret about who was the boss, but tomorrow was Sunday, I thought, and I wouldn't have to deal with him again until Monday afternoon.

When I was putting him away, Gloria's mom's white Impala turned into our road, and pretty soon here they were. Gloria jumped out of the passenger side, and Mrs. Harris opened her door more slowly and then got herself out of the driver's side.

Mrs. Harris was a big woman, at least a head taller than Mom, and older, too, I think. Gloria was an only child, and Mrs. Harris had always treated her, Mom said, like she didn't know the first thing about children and was afraid of them to boot. But she was nice in her awkward way, and she always talked to me as if Mom and I were about the same age. Now she walked over to me and said, "Good morning, Abby. I hope you're well. It's wonderful to see you." She held out her hand, and I offered her mine to shake. She was wearing sunglasses. "I understand you have a new foal, and I would love to be introduced to the young man." She picked up one of her feet to show me her cowboy boot. She always wore red cowboy boots when she came out. I don't think she'd ever been on a horse.

Gloria had always been about my size, that is, not short and not tall, not fat and not thin. I sometimes wondered if we would look like our moms when we got older, and if so, when her future size would kick in, but it hadn't so far, even though lots of the girls had gotten their growth, as my mom would say. Gloria was wearing jeans, a jean jacket, and sneakers. She seemed excited, and that made me excited, too. I said, "They're out. Over here!"

We walked over to the gate, and in a moment, Mom joined us. She and Mrs. Harris had a little hug.

It was quite sunny and warm by now, and the grass in the mares' corral had greened up nicely, because only one mare was out there much. The foal's dam was eating calmly and the foal was stretched out on his side, sleeping, though his little tail flicked against the grass from time to time, and his little ears flicked, too. Mom said, "Follow me. It's time to get acquainted." She opened the gate.

As we walked toward the mare, she looked up at us and then moved around the foal so that she was between him and us. "Perfect," said Mom. She pulled out a handful of carrot pieces. She said, "Okay, girls, now each of you can take some carrots, and we're going to go up to the mare, not the foal, slowly but confidently, and we're just going to feed her some carrots and pet her and pretty much ignore the baby for a while." We did this. The Jewel ate the carrots quite happily, Gloria and I petted her on the face and down the neck, and Mom slipped the halter on her. She said, "Just keep petting her, all over. As if you were brushing her with your hands." We did this, a little carefully, in case she might change her mind about whether she trusted us, but she stood quietly, keeping her eye on the foal but enjoying the petting.

After a little bit, the foal rolled up onto his chest, blinking a little. His eyelashes were really long. He even yawned, which was very cute. Then he got to his feet. This was a production. First he used his front feet to lever himself up, then he got his back feet under him and pushed off and sort of jumped into the air. Then he shook all over and yawned again. Gloria started laughing and her mother said, "Oh, how darling!" but we just kept petting the mare until after a moment, she walked over to him. Mom followed her, holding the lead rope. The foal started to nurse. Mom said, "Okay, now come over here, nice and easy, and start petting her again, on the side away from him, just petting her. We'll see how she likes it."

She liked it fine. The foal nursed and we petted the mare, Gloria and I at the neck and shoulders on the side away from the foal and Mom in front, stroking her face and head. Mom inched her way to the side the foal was on, and then every so often, she let her hand drop smoothly to his shoulder. Then she stroked him lightly but smoothly, so as not to be mistaken for a fly. He did shiver his skin, the way horses do to shake off flies, but after a few minutes, he even stopped doing that. Then she said, "Okay, Abby, trade places with me." I did and then did just what she had done.

The foal's coat wasn't smooth and soft, like the mare's. It was rough and thick, to keep him warm. And he was warm. Because he'd been lying in the sun, his coat was almost hot. I let my fingers stray through it, but smoothly, like Mom had done. At one point, he stopped nursing for a moment and realized that I was next to him. He jumped a little bit, as if startled, which made me jump, too, and that made Gloria jump, and we laughed. I switched places with Gloria. By this time, the colt was more or less used to us being around and even to us petting him, and he didn't seem nervous. In fact, he got bored and walked away, over toward the George corral, just to look at the geldings. Then he jumped in the air and galloped around for a minute or two.

"Now's the test," Mom said. She followed the mare again when the mare followed the colt. We stood there quietly, just the way we had done before, petting the mare and giving her some more carrots. Finally, the colt turned around and looked at us, all standing there. He snorted and jumped, then stopped and looked. Then, the best thing, step by step, he came toward us, toward his mom. His tail kept flicking back and forth. He stopped, took a step or two, stopped again. But finally he was back beside the mare, him on his side and us on our side. He peeked under her neck at us. Mom's hand moved toward his neck and then stroked it. His skin shivered, but he stood still. "Smart boy," said Mom.

"Oh, how lovely," said Mrs. Harris.

"I think that's enough for one day," said Mom.

"I love him," said Gloria. "You are so lucky, Abby."

I knew I was, but I said, "Daddy says that a foal is a terrible responsibility."

"I have every confidence that you are up to it," said Mrs. Harris.

Mom smiled. We went inside for tea, and Gloria and her mom stayed almost until supper. Gloria had a *Seventeen* magazine with her, and we went into my room and sat on the bed and leafed through it. She pointed at a couple of the models and said, "Did I tell you my cousin Emily saw them in Florida at Christmastime? They were sitting together in the restaurant of the hotel where she was staying, and they all had matching outfits on."

"They must have been doing a shoot."

"I guess. Don't you wonder how much they make?"

"I heard it was like a hundred dollars an hour."

"Wow." We stared at the models cavorting in the snow (this was, after all, the February issue), and then Gloria read me the dating column that was written by the guy they had. It was about whether boys like popular girls best or not. As far as I could tell, he wished that they didn't, but he knew that they did. All in all, Gloria and I had a nice afternoon, just the sort of afternoon we had been having ever since we first played Chutes and Ladders in second grade, ever since we got coloring books and her crayon box (forty-eight colors) was always in perfect order. If she broke one, her mom taped it together so all the tips were the same height. My crayon box would be half empty because even though I only liked certain colors, Daddy said I had to use all the colors before I could have a new box. So Gloria would loan me hers and we would color all afternoon. They went home before supper. We hadn't said a word about Stella, and I didn't know if that was good or bad.

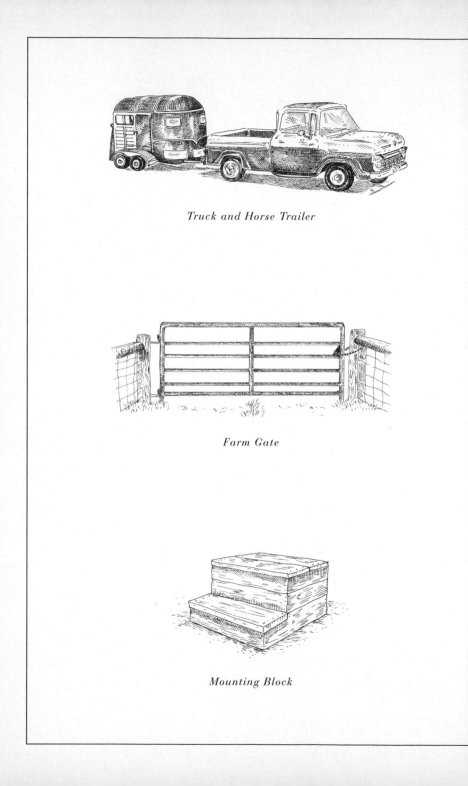

Truck and Horse Trailer

Farm Gate

Mounting Block

Chapter 5

NOW WE COULD MAKE FRIENDS WITH THE COLT, AND WE DID. THE path to a colt's heart is through his mom, and the first thing I did was to make friends with the Jewel (whom I called "Pearl," just between us, as in "Hey, Pearl! Hey, sweet thing! What a good girl you are, Pearl!"). Every time I passed the stall or, if they were out, the corral, I called to Pearl and gave her a couple of pats or a bit of carrot. Pretty soon, she was looking for me and nickering to me. She and the colt stayed out more and more as the weather got better. Mom was cautious about putting the two mares out together with the foal, but the other Jewel didn't mind staying in and eating hay most of the day and then going out at night. I was happy we didn't have any more mares, because that would have meant more stalls to clean.

Daddy started talking about going back to Oklahoma and buying more horses. Horses were cheap in Oklahoma, and there were plenty of them, but now that Danny was out of the house, Daddy hated to leave Mom and me on our own. Then he started talking about whether his brother, Luke, in Oklahoma might bring us some horses, but then Luke would have to be cut in on the profits, and anyway, Luke had a different idea of a good horse from Daddy's idea. Luke was older than Daddy, and though they got along, you never knew whether that would last. Sometimes they didn't fight for a month and sometimes only for a few days. Luke hated for Daddy to "boss him around" or "tell it to him straight" (whichever of these it was depended on your point of view). Whenever they had a fight, Mom said that Daddy felt a strong obligation to witness to Luke, but older brothers, in particular, didn't care to be witnessed to by the boys they had spent a lifetime beating up and bossing around. So, for the time being, there were no horses from Oklahoma. The other thing my mom said once in a while was, "Mark, you should make things up with Danny."

"He needs to work at a hard job for a while and see what life is like."

"If he works long enough, he'll never come back."

"If it's hard enough, he'll learn his lesson."

"You never know what lesson he's learning."

They went round and round like this. But it was a touchy subject, and Mom was careful to not bring it up very often. I think she thought that the idea of horses from Oklahoma and the idea of making up with Danny would come together of

50

their own accord, and better not to push them together before Daddy was ready. In the meantime, she said to me, "You
know your grandfather and his brother Eben didn't speak for
thirteen years because once Eben got drunk and drove home
in the wagon, forgetting your grandfather in town. I don't
think the family ever stopped arguing about what that *meant*.
When you argue about what things *mean*, they just get bigger
and bigger."

The good thing, other than the weather, was that we got a
call from a lady who had horses at the biggest riding stable on
the coast. A girl wanted a pony. The girl was nine, an "ad-
vanced beginner" but small. The lady, who had seen Daddy's
ad in the newspaper, wanted to come out, but Daddy insisted
that it would be his pleasure to trailer the pony to the coast,
and then we spent three days getting ready, which meant not
only cleaning up the pony and me getting out my nicest
English-style riding clothes, it also meant Daddy washing the
truck and the trailer.

"Now, Abby," he said as he did, "this is something you
should know, a business practice. If this lady were to come
out here, she would see our place and she would think that
we really couldn't possibly have a pony that would be good
enough for her client. If we drive there, though, and we are
all cleaned up and shined a bit, then she'll look at our old
truck and trailer and say to herself that she's getting a deal on
the pony, but the fact that everything is spic and span will
tell her that we are *economical* rather than *poor*. She'll be sure
she's getting a good deal on the *right* pony." He suggested that
Gloria come along, and that was fine with me. I knew her

mom would dress her up so that she would look good at the fancy stable.

I'd been polishing the pony with the sweater every day, and even though a gray doesn't shine up as brightly as a chestnut, he looked good and felt good—his coat was as slick as a piece of silk. Daddy could hardly contain himself. He even made Mom iron his jeans on the Friday night before we left.

The stable was about an hour away. I had heard of it but never been there. It wasn't on the way to anywhere, but rather off by itself under a big stand of pines. You had to go through a gate and down a special road to get there. Daddy would have had to pay a dollar just to drive down that road, except that he told the guard he was taking a pony to the stable and the guard waved him past. We drove for a while on the road through a forest—with the windows open, you could smell the pines—but it wasn't cheerful. Fog wafted here and there, and all of the houses were behind big walls and gates. There were, needless to say, no kids playing in the streets. It was like the country but not country. Walls, houses, lawns, and gardens but no animals or fields. Even so, Gloria and I picked out houses—or, rather, mansions—that we thought were pretty.

The lady, who introduced herself as Miss Slater, was waiting for us at the gate to the stable. She was small, not much taller than I, but a little on the wide side. She was wearing copper-colored English-style riding breeches that were wide on top, brown tall boots, and a brown wool jacket. Even though it wasn't that cold, she had gloves on. Daddy stopped the truck and she came to the window with a big smile, which made her look prettier than I thought she had been, and she told us where to park and unload the pony. She gave Gloria and me a nice smile and said to me, "So! You must be Abby! You're going to show us what this pony can do!"

I said, "Yes, ma'am," the way I was supposed to. Daddy opened the back of the trailer and went in. A moment later, he brought out the pony. Miss Slater said, "What's his name?"

Daddy said, "George," with a perfectly straight face.

"Hello, George," said the lady. She put her hands on her hips and stared at the pony while Daddy stood him up. The pony's ears were pricked, and I might have said he was nervous, but he did stand quietly while she walked all around him, then went up to him and picked up his feet and opened his mouth. In the meantime, Gloria and I pretended to be perfectly well-mannered girls and that we were just standing there doing what we'd been told to do, but really we were edging closer and closer toward the gateway to the inner court of the stable so we could get a look.

The whole stable was painted white, and all of the stall doors and windows were painted with dark green trim. Horses' heads looked out over every door, and the courtyard was full of people—some of them were girls or women dressed like Miss Slater, and others were men in overalls who were cleaning stalls. Miss Slater said, "Not bad." I looked at Daddy, who had his poker face on. "Let's see the little fellow go."

I held the pony while Daddy got out the English tack, and Gloria helped him saddle up. When I went to get on, though, the lady said, "Abby, did you bring your hard hat?"

"No, ma'am."

"We'll lend you one. Why don't you lead the pony through here."

We followed her into the courtyard. Everyone there stopped what they were doing and stared at us. The first hard hat she handed me came down over my eyes; the second one sat on my head like a mushroom cap. Gloria started to laugh, but I poked her a good one. Finally, Miss Slater found one—nice black velvet—that fit me. I was relieved. We walked the pony to the mounting block and I got on. Then we went out of the courtyard and over to the arena.

There were five or six horses and riders in the arena—no ponies—and all of them looked at us as I rode George in. Of course, some of the girls said, "Oh, isn't he cute! Look at him!" but I pretended not to hear them. I walked across the arena and then turned left and walked along the rail. The pony flicked his ears here and there, but he minded his manners. After two circuits, we made a little U-turn and went back the other way. Miss Slater called out, "Abby! Please pick up a trot." And so we did. Some horses get into a ring full of other horses and they don't like it because the other horses come too close. Others think that if the ring is full of quiet horses, then every-thing must be okay—no mountain lions anywhere nearby. That was how the pony was. He liked other horses and liked feeling that he didn't have to keep his eye out.

After we had shown off the walk, trot, canter, halt, rein back, and a few turns in either direction, she motioned me into the center, and we trotted over a few poles. Daddy was standing by the rail, chewing on a piece of straw and talking to one of the ladies. I was sure he was putting on his Oklahoma accent so that everyone would think he was the biggest hick in town. We jumped a few low jumps, and then I pulled him up in front of her and said, "Ma'am. Just so you know, he'll jump about anything. Daddy had him jumping over two chairs draped with a tablecloth the other day. He didn't look right or left."

"Hmm," said the lady.

I could tell that she was trying to look undecided, but she seemed happy underneath that, so I knew she liked the pony.

Now she took the rein and led us to the fence, where a girl in fancy riding clothes was sitting. The lady said, "Abby, this is Melinda. She's the girl who's looking for a pony."

Melinda had white eyelashes and big eyes, which made her look like she had just seen a ghost. She reached out and put her fingers on the pony's neck, then she said, in a very low voice, "Is he nice?"

"Oh, sure."

"Is he *always* nice?"

"Well, we've only had him for about six months, but he's always been during that time."

"You're a good rider."

"But he's well behaved anyway." I waved toward Gloria. "She can't ride very well, and he's always fine with her, too."

"My dad thinks I should have a show pony."

I jumped off.

Getting Melinda onto the pony was a big job, as she was practically limp. It was like she could hardly hold herself up as soon as she stepped inside the ring. For one thing, she acted like she was sure one of the other horses might come running at us, and she kept flinching and looking over toward them. The lady gave her a leg up, but as Melinda bent her knee, she sort of crumpled. Finally, since Melinda was small, the lady just put her hands around her waist and set her on the pony. It was Gloria and I who put her feet into the stirrups. The lady fixed the reins in her hands. Melinda closed her eyes for a moment, took a deep breath, and gave the pony a kick. He walked away. He looked a little surprised to see me standing there, knowing that someone was on his back.

The thing was, she wasn't a bad rider. Her heels were down and her thumbs were up and and she sat in the middle of the pony and went with the motion. It was hard to figure out why she was so scared. The pony understood the words "walk," "trot," and "halt" perfectly well and followed every one of the lady's commands. They didn't try a canter. I saw that a life here would be just what a nice pony deserved—not much to do and plenty of time to do it in.

After Melinda got down, Daddy and the lady went off to one side and parleyed for a while, and then he waved me over. He said, "Miss Slater would like to ask you a favor, Abby, dear."

I adopted my most respectful look. She said, "Well, you know, Abby, Melinda's dad would like to see the pony as a good investment, and he is a good investment, but I think he'll need to be shown before Melinda will be ready to show him, so I wonder if you would mind coming over from time to time and taking him in our shows?"

I glanced at Daddy, then said, "I haven't shown English before." I showed western pleasure as a rule.

"But you're a good rider and you say you've jumped the pony a lot, so we can try it. If the pony can't show, I'm afraid that Melinda's father—"

Won't go for it. They didn't have to tell me that. So I nodded. Daddy said, "Miss Slater, that's very kind of you. Abby is eager for all kinds of experience—" and they shook hands. We spent another half an hour with Miss Slater. She gave the pony a real going-over, including holding each leg up really high and then having the pony trot off as soon as she dropped it, but the pony trotted off sound. She looked at his eyes and his teeth again and peered into his ears and ran her fingers the wrong way in his hair to check for funguses or parasites. She even spread apart the hair on the dock of his tail because if a horse has worms, he'll rub his tail. But she didn't find anything, and so she wrote Daddy a check, which he put in his pocket with a serious shake of the hand. It wasn't until we were practically to the gate of the whole area that he started whooping and grinning. Of course, how much he got for the pony wasn't my business or Gloria's, but I knew he'd start bragging about it at some point. All he said to us was, "Well, girls, we can say a prayer of thanks, because the Lord has been good to us today."

Gloria had been my friend for so long that even though she didn't go to our church (and Mom said that, really, they didn't go to any church, unless you called dropping in at St. Dunstan's from time to time "churchgoing"), she never blinked at anything Daddy said about the Lord. All I said was, "Okay." What I was thinking about was going to that horse show to ride the pony. I had heard about it—beautiful horses, and a lot of Thoroughbreds, and everyone perfectly dressed. The horses would have braided manes and tails and sometimes checkerboard patterns combed into their shining rumps. The people would all be wearing velvet hats and their boots would be clean all the way down to the soles, because grooms would prepare the horses. The whole thought made me nervous and excited all of a sudden, especially since I had said yes without really thinking. I let myself imagine it while we were driving through the pines, but then I put it out of my mind as just one of those things that grown-ups say but don't mean.

Daddy was in a good mood for days after the sale of the pony, but I missed the little guy. I didn't think that the girl Melinda felt comfortable enough to really take a liking to him, but I hoped she would at least pet him and give him treats.

In the meantime, now that Daddy had three thousand, five hundred dollars from the sale of a pony he had paid four hundred dollars for, he couldn't wait to get back to Oklahoma and buy some more horses. During this period, he gave me a lot of business tips. For example, when the amount he got for the pony finally came out, he said, "Now, Abby, that extra five hundred dollars we got was because he was gray. Don't forget that. A working horse who's going to live outdoors shouldn't be gray, because that just means that he's going to look dirty all the time—no rancher has the time to wash that horse enough to keep him looking good. But a show horse, and especially a show pony, should be gray, because the judge can't help watching that one just a little longer. A gray show pony stands out, and that's why we got some more money for him. That's a 'premium.'" I don't know that Daddy expected me to go into the horse business when I got older—his sisters got married and never kept up with their riding—but he didn't have Danny to give his tips to any longer, so he gave them to me.

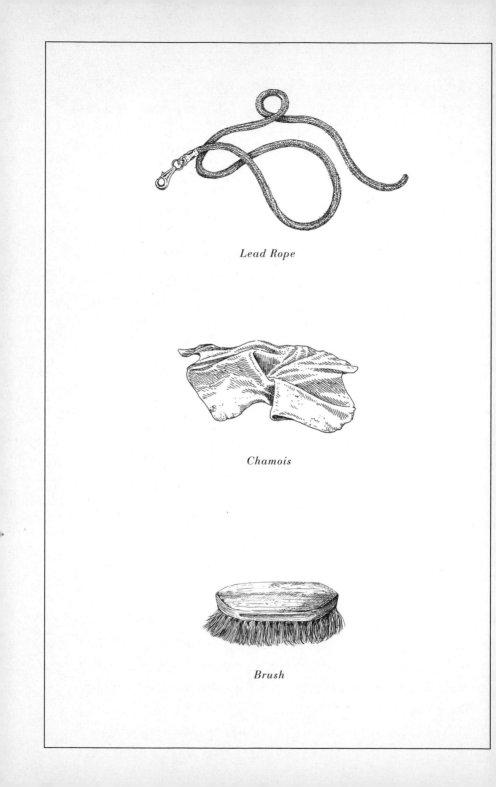

Lead Rope

Chamois

Brush

Chapter 6

WELL, THE MARE DIED. LITTLE JACK WAS A MONTH OLD TO THE day, Daddy was in Oklahoma getting ready to bring the horses back, with Uncle Luke to help him. Mom and I got up Saturday morning to feed the horses.

It wasn't a bad morning—a little chilly, but dry. The first thing we said when we went out the front door was, "Is it too cold for him?" We had left the mare and the foal out for the night. We had done it twice before, because he was getting a little too big for the stall. We decided that it wasn't too cold—he was a big boy and still furry with his foal coat. But as soon as we looked toward the mares' corral, Mom said, "Uh-oh." Normally, they would have been at the gate, waiting for their hay. I said, "Maybe it's all right. Maybe there's enough grass so that she isn't that hungry."

But it wasn't all right. As soon as we got to the top of the hill and looked down, we could see the dark shape of the mare, lying stretched out on her side in the grass, and the foal standing above her, by her rump, poking at her with his nose. While we were running down the hill, she flopped her tail and lifted her head, then tried to lift her front end, but her head fell back into the grass. Jack gave a loud, high whinny, and that was when I started to cry, but we had to keep running anyway.

Mom did some things to try and figure out what was wrong with her—like kneeling down and listening to her belly sounds—but all I did was sit by her head and start to pet her. Even though it was cold, her neck was crusty with dried sweat. Another bad thing was that the hair around the top of her head was worn off, meaning that she would have been rolling around in pain for a long time. But she liked the petting. I stroked her face and ears, and she gave a few grunts and sighs. Mom said, "I think she colicked in the night. Rolling around with the pain might have given her an intestinal twist. Oh, dear. She has no gut sounds at all." Horses always make gut sounds because their digestion is always working.

"She seemed fine when I gave them the hay last night." I always did that around six.

"Oh, there's no telling," said Mom. "What a business." Then she said, "Hey, darlin', does your tummy hurt?"

I kept petting Pearl's head and her neck, and she closed her eyes. In the meantime, the foal came over to me and began to nose my shoulder. I felt his breath on my cheek and twisted around to pet him, too, but he moved away and went back to pushing on the mare and whinnying to her.

"I'm sure he's terribly hungry," said Mom.

"Are you going to call the vet?"

Daddy hated it if we had to call the vet, even though sometimes we did. He maintained that he knew almost as much as most vets, and when they came and said, "Well, Mark, I don't really know what to tell you," you still had to pay them anyway.

Mom was stroking Pearl on the belly, long, kind strokes that the mare seemed to like. At any rate, her eyes were still closed. She said, "Abby, sweetheart, I don't know what the vet could do. Look how swollen her belly is. That means the gases have already built up and the poisons have started to break down her insides. There's nothing he could do that would save her. Honey, I hate to have to tell you this, but she's going to die, and what we have to do is just keep her company. Do you understand that?"

I said, "Yeah. Yes, I do."

She nodded. After a moment, she said, "Okay."

So, we knelt by the mare for a few minutes, Mom stroking her belly and me stroking her head, and she seemed to quiet down and relax. I played with her mane a bit, too. Horses like you to scratch them lightly at the base of their manes, because that's a spot they can't reach themselves. But we couldn't do anything with Jack. He was restless. He kept pushing at her and pawing the ground. Once in a while, he would take a few strands of grass between his lips, but then he would toss his head and spit them out. All the time he was making noise—

little whinnies and nickers and grunts. He went around her a few times.

At one point, he stood behind her tail, reaching across her back leg, trying to nurse from her. He knew where the spot was, but since she was lying down, he couldn't make it work. I was just on the verge of saying to Mom, "Maybe I should—" but I didn't know what I should do, when the mare lifted her head and her shoulders. Mom and I backed away—there was no telling what she would do—and she heaved herself up, shoulders first. She rolled up on her breast and got her front legs under her and then made herself stand up. She gave a huge grunt, almost a groan. When she was up, she spread her legs to each side and kind of staggered in place. Mom was behind me, and she put her hands on my shoulders as if I were going to go and help the mare and she was going to stop me.

The mare stood there with her head down and her ears flopped, and the foal went to his accustomed spot and started to nurse. But it only lasted a minute. She couldn't do it. She began to collapse, and the foal jumped out of the way. When she hit the ground, her eyes were already closed, and I think she died a minute or two later. By that time I was crying so hard I couldn't see, and Mom was crying, too. We got down next to her and petted her and petted her. The foal kept whinnying.

After a little bit, Mom leaned over and listened to her chest, and then she sat up. "Honey, I'm going to get the foal's halter."

When she was gone, I sat back on my heels and looked at the mare. What had happened to her was invisible. Everything about her looked nice—her furry ears, her hooves, her shiny coat, her long tail. I thought of Daddy saying, "The Lord works in mysterious ways." That certainly seemed to be true in this case. I wiped my eyes with my sleeve a couple of times. I couldn't believe two things—how fast it all happened and how soundly we had slept all night when a hundred yards from the house, the mare was dying and the foal was—what? Terrified? Out of his mind? I didn't know.

Mom came back with the halter and the lead rope. It took her a while to get the halter on Jack, because he was throwing his head and putting his nose down to touch the mare—he was very upset—but Mom was patient, and she talked to him in a low voice. She tried over and over, but when it didn't work, she just kept talking and trying. When she finally had it on him, we had to lead him uphill away from the mare. He didn't want to go. He would turn his head and whinny or stop and try to go back, but Mom wouldn't let him. She didn't exactly pull, but she didn't let him go back, either.

My job was to walk alongside him, pushing him a little if he needed it, but otherwise just petting him and keeping him company. We had taught him to lead, so he went along well enough, but there was a terrible racket of whinnies and nickers, and I couldn't believe how sad the sounds made me. I hated to leave the mare by herself down there, even though, as Daddy would have said, she was "happily departed." We got Jack to the top of the hill, through the gate, and into the stall. Then Mom went into the house and brought out a big metal bowl and a half gallon of milk. I was standing outside the stall, leaning against the door, watching him rocket around in there, if anything more panicky than he had been.

We hadn't taken his halter off, so Mom set down the bowl and the milk outside the stall and went in and caught him, snapping the lead rope back on his halter. Then she brought him to the door and said, "Pour some milk in the bottom of the bowl. Not too much. And bring it in." Jack stood next to her, but he kept nodding. I don't think he knew what he was doing.

Mom held him while I brought the bowl to his lips. As soon as I touched the milk to his muzzle, he started smacking them together, but then he put his head up. Mom said, "He doesn't realize that milk is for drinking—he thinks it's for suckling. He's a baby. He'll learn, though. Just hold it still." The bowl wasn't heavy, and there wasn't much milk in it, so I held it as steadily as I could. For the first while, every time Jack got a taste of the milk, he would root upward, but then he learned to drink it (he had already learned to drink water, of course), and pretty soon, he had taken all the milk. Mom said, "Pour out some more. We'll give him a little. But he has to get used to cow's milk, so we can't give him all he wants just yet."

In the end, he probably drank about half a quart. Then Mom brought him some nice grass hay, not so much for him to eat, though a month-old foal would have tried a little of his mom's hay from time to time—but more for him to play with.

By the time we had fed the Georges and the other mare (who was plenty interested in what was going on), I was exhausted. Mom was, too. All we had for breakfast was some Rice Krispies and an orange to split.

There was no calling Daddy—he was somewhere between Oklahoma and California with Uncle Luke and six horses, and unless something went wrong, he wouldn't call us. Mom didn't expect him until Sunday night. And she didn't expect the truck from the rendering plant until Monday morning. "At least it's pretty cold," she said.

We went down the hill with a couple of old horse blankets and laid them over the body of the mare.

We fed Jack a little more of the milk. Otherwise, I stood outside his stall and watched him. He continued to be restless, and much of the time he just stared over the door of his stall, which he also kicked with his knees. I was sure he thought she would be coming up the hill any minute. When he was standing still, I approached him very quietly and started petting him on the neck, first little tickles and light brushings. He seemed to like that, so I made firmer and smoother strokes, down and down and down, and all the time saying, "It's going to be all right, little guy. You'll be all right." I did it on one side of his neck and then on the other. He seemed to like it. I liked it. I didn't really want to do anything else. Even though I had three horses to ride and my room to clean before the end of Saturday, I didn't want to do anything but be with Jack.

When Daddy and Uncle Luke got home, with two geldings and four mares in Uncle Luke's big rig, Daddy was not happy about the death of Pearl, but since he didn't see it, he was more mad than sad. He wasn't mad at me or Mom—we had done our best—he was just mad, or mad again, at the man who had sold him a pregnant mare in the first place.

During the course of the month since Jack's foaling, Daddy had come around to accepting the colt and agreeing that he was a pretty boy—a very pretty boy. He had also looked under the mare's upper lip and found a tattoo, which meant that she was a registered Thoroughbred and had run in races. There was no telling what her real name was, but if we wanted to, we could use the tattoo number to trace her and find out who her sire and dam were and if she had won any money. That was fun to think about, and once Daddy even said, "So maybe we've got another Whirlaway here." Normally, he never let himself think like this about a horse, because gambling was a sin and in lots of states a crime, and horse racing itself was as "crooked as your elbow" (though some of the tracks were very beautiful), but he would never deny that Thoroughbreds were a sight to see, whether they were running or jumping or just romping around in the corral, like Jack. But now the mare had died, and if the whole foal thing had been upsetting before, now it was a real pain in the neck.

And, of course, until the rendering truck came for Pearl, there was no place to put the new mares other than into stalls, which meant straw and cleaning and restlessness—after such a long ride, what they really needed was a chance to walk around and eat some grass. Daddy had planned to put the Georges and the mare and foal in for the night, divide up the new set into mares and geldings, and let them have the pastures until morning, but he didn't want the new mares seeing the dead mare. When I asked him why, he said it was "just not good. Bad way to introduce them to the place." And so there was more work—the geldings outside and six horses in for the night, including Jack, who was still staring and whinnying, but not as badly. We had fed him the milk ten times by then and watched him closely. He seemed okay, but the vet would have to look at him, just to be sure he was all right with it, and all right in general, when he came out to give all the new horses a once-over.

Uncle Luke was not born again. He and Daddy had always gone to the same church, and then Daddy accepted Jesus into his life and went to a different church. Uncle Luke didn't quite understand the difference between the churches or didn't care about the difference. Daddy felt a call to witness to Uncle Luke, but most of the time he kept it to himself. Uncle Luke was older than Daddy by about four years (Uncle John came in between them; he had died as a boy when a mule kicked him in the head), but he was shorter than Daddy by about four inches. He was bowlegged and almost bald. He always wore a bandanna tied around his head and a Stetson on top of that. He had a big silver buckle he'd won roping in the rodeo. His boots had purple morning glories tooled into the leather, and he always wore them because he said that you didn't want to die before you wore out your best pair of boots.

On Monday morning, after the truck came and took the mare away, and after we gave the foal some milk, and while we were waiting for the vet, Uncle Luke said to me, "Abby, let's see you ride a couple of these cayuses." I knew I was going to have to ride all day, because it was a teacher conference day at school, and we had the day off.

I got on Jewel first (Jewel Number 1, since now we had Number 2, Number 3, Number 4, and Number 5, which we named Red Jewel, Blue Jewel, Star Jewel, and Roan Jewel). I showed off her gaits, her stops, her spins, and her figure eights. Uncle Luke leaned on the fence smoking a cigarette. Each time he finished one, he stubbed it out with the toe of his boot, picked it up, broke off the tip, ground the tip between his fingers to make sure it was cool and put the cigarette butt in his pocket. Then he lit up another one by striking a kitchen match against the fence. He blew on the tip of the match until it was cool and broke off the tip and put the two halves in his pocket, too. Finally, I pulled the Jewel up right next to him, and I said, "Uncle Luke, it looks to me like smoking is a full-time job for you. I don't see why you just don't quit."

He laughed. "Quitting would kill me, Miss Abby. I know it, so why chance it?"

"Daddy quit."

"And that was a sight to behold. Put me off of quitting for good. Go get on that other bay. He's a lot better-looking than this nag."

"She's nice."

"I didn't say she wasn't, darlin'. But she's got no spark. Let's see that bay. What's your Dad call the geldings?"

"George. But he lets me call the foal Jack."

"That's big of him."

I ignored this and went to get Ornery George.

While Daddy was gone to Oklahoma, Ornery George and I had gotten along well enough by me skirting all the issues between us. If he was willing to trot but he didn't want to put in more effort to trot out, I let him go at his own pace and more or less got him to go a little faster when he didn't seem to be paying attention. It worked like this—we would be walking. I would kick him up into a trot and he would poke along. If I pushed him, he would pin his ears and switch his tail. Then we would come around the corner of the arena so that we were heading toward the barn, and he would pick up speed, at which point I would give him another kick, and since he was already going faster, he would give me a little extra, which would last almost around the far end, too. Or if I smacked him with the quirt and he kicked because he didn't like it, I would pretend that he really didn't need to be smacked with the quirt again. Riding him made my stomach hurt, but I kept that to myself, another secret Ornery George and I had together.

I went and got him. Uncle Luke helped me brush him off and tack him up, taking a ten-minute break from smoking to do so. Then he offered me a leg up and threw me into the saddle. He said, "Honey, you are light as a feather."

Ornery George started out in a pretty good mood—it wasn't that he was always lazy, it was that he always wanted to do things his way, and then sometimes his way and my way coincided. We did a few of the same exercises that I had done with the mare—walk, jog, lope, some stops, a spin one direction and then the other direction, and then a fairly large figure eight, with lead changes in the middle. Uncle Luke said, "He's a good-looking thing, but he doesn't have the happiest expression on his face. From that I take it that he's not the most eager-to-please animal in the world."

I shook my head. I thought we were having a fairly good day, though. Just then, Ornery George tried to veer for the gate, because he had decided that he was finished. The veer wasn't much, and I pulled him over, but then I gave him a smack with the quirt, just because, ordinarily, that's what you would do to say, "Not yet."

At that, Ornery George started bucking, and he leapt and twisted like a rodeo horse, at least seven or eight big bucks and kicks, with his head between his knees. When I jerked his head out from between his knees and pulled it around, he got it back down there and kept going. I had to hold the horn of my saddle and sit back, but even then he almost got me off. He hadn't had me off in over a month. Finally, Uncle Luke managed to get to us. Ornery George was almost finished, anyway—I could feel it in his body. Uncle Luke grabbed the reins just below the bit, and he said, "*What* the hell do you think you're doing, Mr. Horse?" He gave Ornery George a jerk, and the horse's head shot into the air and he started to back up. Uncle Luke gave him another jerk, and he stopped. His eyes were big and his ears were forward. Uncle Luke said, "Someone doesn't know who the boss is."

"That's true. I—"

"Honey, it's not your job to tell him who the boss is. Your daddy should have made that clear to him months ago."

"He said that wouldn't work."

"Oh, sure it will—"

Just then, Daddy came around the barn and shouted, "Vet's here! Need some help!"

Uncle Luke said, "You walk him out now, and he and I will come to a little understanding tomorrow or the next day when your dad's away for a bit. You got school tomorrow?"

I said, "Yeah, of course."

"Well, we'll have a little school after school."

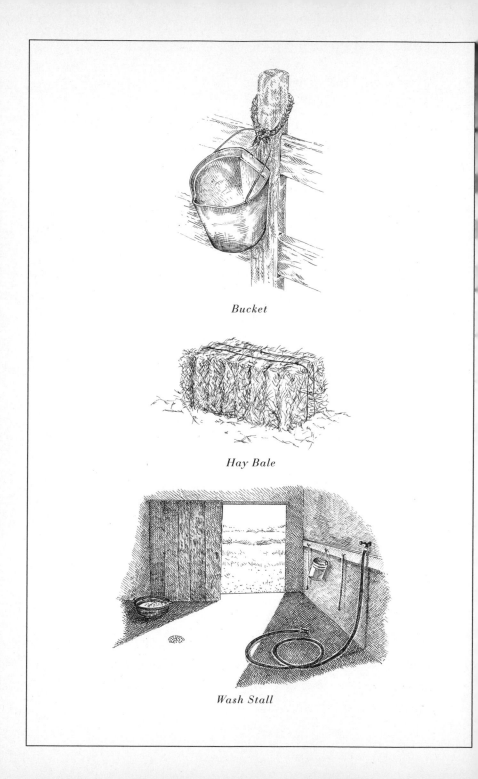

Bucket

Hay Bale

Wash Stall

Chapter 7

ON TUESDAY, WE COULDN'T RIDE BECAUSE OF THE POURING RAIN, and on Wednesday, both Mom and Daddy were gone to the chapel to set up chairs for the evening service, which every family had to do in turn—it was our time about once every eight or nine weeks, though if one of the old ladies had to do it, Mom would go and help.

It was therefore a perfect day for Uncle Luke to take Ornery George in hand, as he said. I rode Jewel Number 1 and gave the foal some milk as soon as I got home, and then Uncle Luke helped me with Ornery George. We had a lot more horses to ride now, but the plan was to let them get settled until Friday and begin them Saturday. Uncle Luke was to stay through the weekend and help with that, then go back to Oklahoma. That was why he had brought his own saddle.

It took us about ten minutes to get Ornery George brushed and tacked. Uncle Luke led him into the arena, stood him up, and stepped up on him. Ornery George flicked his ears. He knew perfectly well that he had a different rider, and I knew perfectly well that he would put Uncle Luke to the test sooner or later.

They got on fine for about fifteen minutes. Uncle Luke made George walk up briskly and trot in both directions. It wasn't until the first lope, to the right, that George gave any trouble—I saw him do it. When Uncle Luke asked for the lope, George flicked his ears backward and humped his back. Uncle Luke smacked him with the end of the reins and said, "Get on, now." George didn't respond. This time, Uncle Luke both flicked the reins and spurred him. George pinned his ears, stuck his head down, and bucked. Uncle Luke spurred and smacked him again. George bucked some more. At that point, Uncle Luke did something I'd heard about but never seen—he vaulted out of the saddle, landed on his feet, bent his knees, and set his heels, pulling the horse around with one rein. He made the horse go around a couple of times, and then George stopped moving. But he looked happy. He looked like he thought Uncle Luke had come off because he'd bucked him off.

Uncle Luke walked the horse over to me and handed me the reins. He said, "Bit of a rogue. But we'll work it out of him."

He went into the barn and came out with a coiled rope.

Both Daddy and Uncle Luke had learned how to rope cattle when they were boys, but Daddy hardly did it at all anymore. Uncle Luke, though, still hired out to do ranch work, and he roped cattle all the time. Now he came over and held out his hand for the reins. Then he led George into the center of the arena. George went along nicely.

"Now, Abby," said Uncle Luke, "this is a horse who's had his own way over and over. And underneath that is some stubbornness of temperament. All horses have something— stubbornness or fear or selfishness. Ideally, you'd fix that early on, but a horse who's had several owners, that's a sign that the stubbornness or whatever never got fixed. This horse thinks he's the boss now." He uncoiled a loop of the rope and laid it on the ground. It was big enough so that a moment later he could lead George forward until he had both hind feet in the loop. Uncle Luke then lifted the loop up and brought it over George's tail and haunches so that it came to rest around his loins, just behind the saddle. He slipped off George's bridle and hung it on the fence. Now Uncle Luke tightened the rope. George stood there, his ears flicking sus-piciously. Uncle Luke tightened the rope again and pulled on it. All of a sudden, George pinned his ears, gave a big buck, kicked out, put his head down, and started throwing himself around as if the rope were a mountain lion on his back and he had to get it off.

Uncle Luke hung on to the rope and George pulled him around the arena with him. Every time the horse bucked, the rope tightened around his belly. The idea, I could see, was to make bucking so painful that the horse would stop. But George was stubborn, and it took so long I began to get scared. They kicked up a lot of dust. Uncle Luke's hat fell off.

By the time they were finished, the horse had bucked thirty times or more. The saddle was cockeyed, and both of them were panting and sweaty. Uncle Luke pulled the bandanna off his head and wiped his face, then went and picked up his hat.

George just stood there, his sides heaving and his head down. Uncle Luke took a deep breath, coiled up some of the rope, pulled once on the horse. George didn't move. Uncle Luke went over to him with the bridle and put it on him, then he loosened the rope and lifted it over his tail. When it was a loop on the ground again, he stepped the horse out of it, picked it up, and hung it over a fence post. Then he uncinched the saddle and straightened it, cinched it back up. George didn't move except when asked. Uncle Luke walked him around in a couple of small circles, then stood him up and mounted again. He gave George a kick and said, "Move off, now."

George moved off, and I let out my breath. He was still breathing hard—his nostrils were flared and his sides were going in and out. They must have walked about, here and there, for ten minutes. Uncle Luke even had a cigarette, right up on the horse. I was about to go into the house and get a drink of water when Uncle Luke urged George up into a trot and then into a lope. George gave him about a minute, and then he put his head down again, dropped Uncle Luke over his shoulder, spun on his haunches, and galloped to the other end of the arena, leaving Uncle Luke sitting there. Uncle Luke got up and went and picked up his hat. I was beginning to get scared.

Uncle Luke had a smile on his face, but he wasn't happy. He went over to George, took the rein that was dangling down, and brought him over to where I was standing. He handed me the rein.

I said, "Uncle Luke, are you mad?"

"Course not. But I am resolute. You'll never get anywhere with a horse if you get mad."

He went over to the fence and took the coil of rope.

Then he came back to me and said, "You ever see your dad lay a horse down?"

"You mean for the vet?"

"No, I mean to teach him submission."

I said, "No."

"Well, it's an interesting thing to watch."

In the meantime, George was the one who was watching, and as soon as Uncle Luke took the reins out of my hand, he started backing away. Uncle Luke just followed him, but as he was doing so he uncoiled his rope and all of a sudden flicked it over George's foot so that it caught him around the ankle. George noticed this and stopped, just for a moment, but then he backed up another couple of steps. Uncle Luke tossed the rope up over the horn of the saddle and then pulled on it a little so that George had to pick his foot up. At this point, George reared up and struck out with the untied foot. Uncle Luke ducked out of the way. George was snorting. He reared up again, and when he came down, Uncle Luke pulled up his foot with the rope and George fell over onto his side. He struggled once to get up, but Uncle Luke kept hold of his foot with the rope and he couldn't manage it. When George was flat out, Uncle Luke went over and sat down on his shoulder, right in front of the saddle. George lifted his head but then dropped it down again. After that, they just sat there for a few minutes.

The dust settled in the arena.

Uncle Luke pulled out a cigarette and a match and lit up, sitting there. Then, while he was smoking the cigarette, he sang, "Old Stewball was a racehorse, and I wish he were mine. He never drank water. He always drank wine." The song had about four verses. When Uncle Luke had sung all of them and finished his cigarette and put his match and his butt back in his pocket, he stood up.

George lay there quietly, making no effort to move, and Uncle Luke then patted him on the head and said, "There's a good son. Just like that." Finally, he shook the reins and the horse got to his feet. He was trembling, and he looked exhausted. Uncle Luke walked him around again for a minute or two, then mounted him. He didn't ride him much—a little walk, trot, and lope, but George did as he was told. When he got off, Uncle Luke called me over. He said, "Now, Abby, look at his eye. He doesn't have that balky look anymore. This horse was keeping himself to himself all along. That's not his job, and, as he showed you, it's dangerous to boot. I think now he knows who's boss."

I nodded, the way you do when adults tell you something. I surely didn't think I would ever be able to do that to a horse. By the time Mom and Daddy got home from setting up the church, we had George cooled out and brushed off and put in the gelding corral with the others, who all seemed to be getting along well enough.

*　*　*

While Mom cooked dinner, I went into Jack's stall and did a thing I had started doing, which was to pet him all over, ears to tail, just long firm strokes along his neck and back and sides. He stood stock-still for it. I didn't know why I did it, except that he seemed to like it—he didn't move away—and I liked it. I wasn't picking up his feet or trying to get him to do anything or training him. It only took five minutes or so, but I did it every time I gave him his milk. On this particular day, I told him that he was never going to be the sort of horse who needed to be laid down. He was going to be a good horse from the beginning, which was right that minute.

In the days since the death of the mare, Jack had settled down for the most part, but it was still a question what to do with him. He was just over a month old, and he needed a friend. Daddy said that maybe the pony could have been his friend, but the pony was gone. None of the mares or geldings could really be trusted. The mares would probably not like him, and if they didn't, they could kick him hard and really hurt him. With geldings, you never knew. And, he said, "It's not like I have time to sit and watch them all the time and make sure nothing happens. And neither do you."

But Jack couldn't go on the way he was, which was living in a stall and going out into one of the corrals for an hour every day while the others were brought in. Foals on stud farms were out all the time, at least in nice weather. I even heard Daddy tell Mom that we should give him away, but I saw her shush him, and then I suppose they prayed about it.

Jesus was merciful, because, at least for the time being, we didn't give him away. Instead, Uncle Luke, seeing our predicament, proposed that he and Daddy spend a day building a new corral—not as big as the others, but big enough for three or four horses to trot around in for a bit. "Give you way more flexibility. And the ground's soft enough. We can get those postholes dug in no time." To me, Uncle Luke said, "Your daddy didn't get to be this stubborn all by himself, so I feel obliged to do what I can for you, Abby, because I know you like that little guy." When I came home from school Friday afternoon, they had all the posts in the ground, and while I was riding the mare and working around the other mares, they ran the woven wire fencing.

They worked until after dark, and we had a late supper. I would say that everyone was happy. Daddy let Uncle Luke smoke at the table (though Mom opened the kitchen windows so the air blew through), and the two of them talked about snakes back in Oklahoma. They both had stories. Daddy had found a rattler in a bag of grain. Uncle Luke had found a rattler in his bed. Daddy had gone for a swim once in the crick below their house, and a cottonmouth had swum right alongside him, round and round. That was nothing, Uncle Luke had been climbing a tree and saw a rope hanging from a high branch, and when he reached up to grab it, it was a rattler. If Uncle Luke thought that was something, well, Daddy had roped a snake. How about this, Uncle Luke had *used a snake as a rope*. Of course, by now we were all laughing, it was really late, and pretty soon we went to bed.

In the morning, first thing, I gave Jack his milk and his petting session, and then I put him out in the new pen with some hay and a water bucket tied to a corner post. He romped and played and seemed to know that this was all for him. I still wished he had a friend, though.

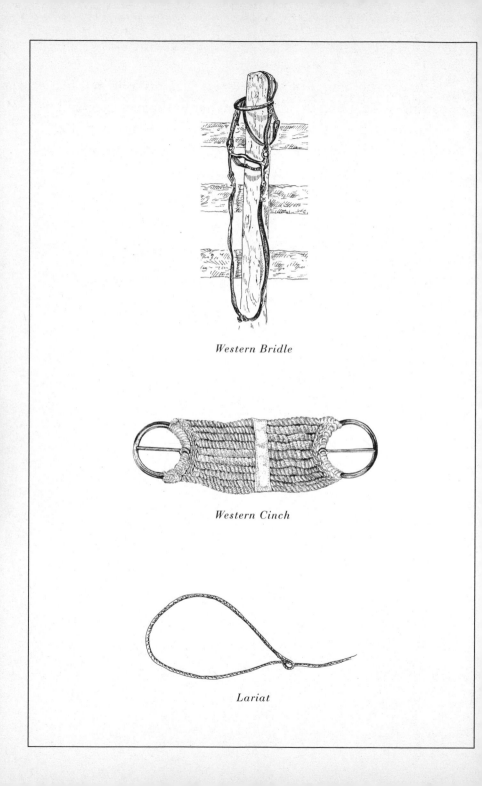

Western Bridle

Western Cinch

Lariat

Chapter 8

Over the weekend, we worked with the new horses. I could tell they had been pretty cheap, because all the things you could fix needed fixing—they all required shoeing, or, if they didn't have shoes, their feet were broken and untrimmed. Their tails were tangled and their manes were too long, and most of them were only partly shed out, with dull, uneven coats that we had to scrape with the shedding blade or, according to Uncle Luke, a farrier's rasp, but we didn't have that. The vet had checked their teeth—two of them would have to have their teeth worked on, which meant that the vet had to come back out and file off sharp corners. It was a time-consuming job, but afterward, they would be more comfortable eating and would get the benefit of their feed, which, since feed was expensive and no one wanted to buy a horse in poor condition (except Daddy, who could always see beneath the surface), was worth it in the end. Still, they seemed well mannered enough.

And they looked different Monday morning from how they looked Friday morning, because we worked all Saturday, and then Uncle Luke declined to accompany us to our church on Sunday. He said he would go to the regular Baptist church in town, but there was no way to tell whether he had or not. Even so, he didn't mind working Sundays, and so he did pull manes and give baths all afternoon. Daddy might have said something about it being against the Lord's day, but, as he pointed out, it wouldn't have made a difference, anyway.

It was good to have Uncle Luke around, but when he drove away in his big rig early Monday morning, we were happy to see him go, because he did make it a point to do things his way and to be sure that Daddy knew he was doing things his way.

That afternoon, I got on Ornery George for the first time since his session with Uncle Luke. Daddy was grooming one of the new geldings—we called him "Black George"—so that I could get off Ornery George and right onto that one with only a switching of the saddle. He didn't see that when I threw the saddle onto Ornery George's back, he pinned his ears and reached around as if to bite me. He had never done that before, but anyway, he didn't bite me. He was just showing me that he could. I led Ornery George to the mounting block. I put my foot in the stirrup, grabbed his mane, and began to hoist myself on when Ornery George leapt away from the block and deposited me in the dirt. I was okay except I sat on my left hand. I jumped up. I still had Ornery George's rein in my right hand, and I gave him a jerk. He started backing up and pulling me with him. I gave him another jerk. Daddy tied Black George to the bar and came trotting over, and when Ornery George kept backing up, even though I was jerking the rein, he took the rein out of my hand. Ornery George stopped and stood still.

Daddy said, "What's going on with you, buddy? Got a thorn in your cinch?" He leaned down and put his hand inside the cinch and felt around. George flinched away from him. Daddy said, "Come on, buddy, come on, buddy," and started leading him forward. George walked along nicely enough. Only when Daddy turned toward him did the horse throw his head. Daddy walked him over to the arena, opened the gate, took off the bridle, and let George go. George bucked like mad all around the arena, stopping only a little bit in order to run a few strides and start bucking again. Daddy leaned on the fence. Finally, he said, "Well, you've got to wonder what's got into him."

As for me, I couldn't help thinking that it was rather interesting that what Uncle Luke had done with George had never been mentioned in the five intervening days, certainly not by me. Daddy often said, "All secrets are guilty secrets." I said, "Did Uncle Luke tell you he rode the horse?"

"No, he did not," said Daddy. "I did not give him permission to ride the horse. Did you?"

"I didn't know he needed permission."

"Well—" He looked at me. "Did he sack him out? Lay him down?"

I said, "I guess so. He said he needed to learn his lesson."

"And then he left before you could find out what lesson, exactly, it was that he learned."

I said, "I guess so."

"Well, Abby, it looks to me like the horse learned the wrong lesson. What do you think?"

"I don't want to ride him."

"I don't blame you."

"Are you mad?"

"Not at you."

"At George?"

"Of course not."

All of this time, George had been bucking and kicking out, but now he settled and stood across the arena with his head down. Daddy whistled with his fingers between his teeth, and George looked up. Then he turned toward us and walked, then trotted, to the gate. Daddy said, "Put a halter on him and walk him around the arena for ten minutes, because now we have to start all over with him." He stopped, then said, "Abby. He's not a bad horse. I'm going to tell you something about the horse business. You see how we are giving this horse another chance?"

I nodded.

"It's because he's good-looking. When you go to buy a horse someday, you make sure he or she is good-looking. They live longer because they get more chances to redeem themselves. You hear me?"

"Yes, sir."

"And another thing. Anything you saw your uncle, bless

his soul, do with this horse, you just forget it. Put it out of your mind. Got that?"

I nodded at that, too.

While I was walking Ornery George, he behaved well enough. But he was jittery and I had to go so carefully to get the saddle off that it took me ten minutes. The Ornery George I knew had been grumpy. This Ornery George was nutty.

I rode Roan Jewel and Blue Jewel. They were nice enough. Then I went to the pen and gave Jack his milk. After he drank it, he stood with his head down and his ears flopped while I ran a chamois over him, head to tail, on both sides. We often used the chamois on the horses just to shine them up, but on him I used the rough side, which seemed to give him a nice scratching. While I was doing this, standing back by his shoulder, his head came around my body. I thought he was looking for something, a bit of hay, maybe, but he didn't seem to be. I finished rubbing him with the chamois and picked up the bowl. He followed me to the gate, and I patted him on the nose after I had let myself out. Later, when we were giving all the horses their alfalfa for the night, Daddy said, "That foal gave you a hug."

"He did?"

"That was a horse hug."

I thought about that later, in bed. Horses normally show their appreciation by nickering at you, or pricking their ears when you come, or, to be frank, getting inside your space and crowding you, and then you have to shoo them away, because they have to respect you even though you weigh about a tenth

89

of what they do. I had never felt a horse do that thing before that Daddy said was a hug, just that steady pressure for a moment or two that said something like, "Be next to me."

That kid, Brian Connelly, was now calling Stella every night and talking to her for at least forty-five minutes. Every day at lunch, she bragged about how she hardly had the time to do her homework because he was bothering her so much. And then, first thing in the morning, he would stand with her by her locker while she sorted her books for the day and talk to her some more. Gloria and I sometimes found ourselves waiting for her, and for the life of me, I couldn't understand why he talked about all the things he did. For example, he would have watched a show on TV the night before, something everyone watched, like *Dick Van Dyke*. I was the only person in my class who didn't watch *Dick Van Dyke*, because we didn't have a TV. But Brian wasn't talking to me, he was talking to Stella, and he would tell her everything that happened in a show that she herself had seen, including all the jokes, which he would laugh at with his mouth open. Or he would tell her what he had for breakfast (usually Wheaties but sometimes a crispy fried egg "because I don't like it all runny").

Gloria and I would stand there watching Stella while Brian talked to her. She kept this happy expression on her face all the time and nodded. Gloria once said to me, "Look at her, she's nodding to the rhythm, like he's singing a song. I don't think she's hearing what he's saying." After that, I couldn't see the nodding in any other way—though when you asked Stella what Brian had said, she knew.

I can't say that he wasn't interested in her, because sometimes he asked her questions—what shows had she seen the
night before? What had she had for breakfast? What was that
thing she was wearing called (in this case, a "dickey," which
was a knitted turtleneck that you could wear under your shirt
to keep your neck warm, and you didn't have to have the
whole sweater, but in that case, what was the point, I thought),
or what was the plaid of her skirt called? When Brian was in a
question-asking mood, he asked questions until you wanted to
pop him one. And, in fact, when we were in elementary
school, he had been popped more than once, which at the time
had made me feel sorry for him.

Now that he was so interested in Stella, though, I could
kind of see Brian the way those mean kids had seen him back
then. Fact was, Brian was big now, and those kids weren't, yet,
so Brian did pretty much what he pleased. He also got good
grades, always sat in the front row in class, and always "con-
tributed," so the teachers liked him. Stella said, "He's kind of
important, isn't he?" and Gloria and I didn't tell her any different. In fact, I would say that Stella saw herself and Brian as the
most popular couple in our grade, which didn't sit well with
the Big Four. From my point of view, Stella's concentration on
Brian meant that she expected me as much as Gloria to listen
to the "Tales of Brian" and learn something. What we learned
about, mostly, was getting dressed, since she was very careful to
dress nicely every day, and she never wore the same thing more
than once in two weeks. One of Gloria's jobs, which I didn't
have to share, was to go shopping with Stella and her mother,
looking for more and more clothes. These were clothes that

she could offer to share but didn't have to, since she was two sizes bigger than both Gloria and me. At our school, nobody wore very nice clothes, especially in the winter, when it was cold, rainy, and muddy. I could see the Big Four looking at Stella and rolling their eyes, but I didn't feel I could say anything to Stella. Gloria shrugged and said that they should mind their own business.

One day, Stella wore stockings.

It was only March and way too chilly and damp for stockings, and anyway, girls in the seventh grade didn't wear stockings to school. We wore loafers and kneesocks in the winter and sneakers and kneesocks or ankle socks in the warmer months. At that point, I had never even worn stockings, and Gloria had worn them only once, to her cousin's wedding, with a pair of dyed satin flats. Stella wore them with flats, too—navy blue with little bows on them—and a knee-length navy skirt, a round collared blouse, and a navy cardigan with little red cats all over it.

Brian, of course, noticed the stockings right away, and he kept looking at them. First thing in the morning, I heard him say, "Those look nice," and Stella just smiled and rubbed her hand down her calf, as if smoothing the nylon. She said, "They're warmer than they look, really." She pranced around in them for the rest of the morning.

But then, as Stella was walking into the lunchroom, with Brian right behind her, Mary A. ripped her stocking with a pencil point, and then said, "Oh! Look what happened! I am so sorry!" But Stella's stocking had a big gaping hole in it, and now it sagged down. Mary A. was grinning.

Stella jumped back and said, "You are not sorry! You did that on purpose!"

"How dare you say that!" exclaimed Mary A., and then the other three started exclaiming, too—how dare she, what a thing to say, who did she think she was, all that sort of thing meant to make Stella out as the bad one and Mary out as the good one. Brian wasn't saying anything for once, just standing there gawking, and I stepped forward, but Gloria poked me and shook her head. She was right. It wasn't a good idea to attract the attention of the Big Four, especially when they were in full cry already. Stella dropped her tray on one of the tables and ran out of the lunchroom. After a moment or two, Gloria and I went after her. I saw Barbara and Alexis Goldman watch us leave the lunchroom and then turn to each other and shake their heads. Stella was in the girls' bathroom, and she was bawling.

There wasn't any blood, and at first I didn't understand why she was crying like that. The Big Four had been mean, and maybe that was enough, but what Stella was saying was, "Look at it! It's ripped! It's terrible! I have to go home, I can't wear this. They're ruined!"

I said, "The other one's okay."

"It isn't!" exclaimed Stella, and then she pulled up her skirt. That was the first pair of panty hose that I ever saw, and yes, if one leg was ruined, the whole thing was ruined. Then Stella said. "My mom is going to kill me, because she bought these for going to my aunt's wedding, and they were *exPENsive!*"

"Well, you better take them off," said Gloria. "You can't wear them that way."

The bell rang for class. Nobody else came into the girls' bathroom. Stella made us wait until all the noise in the hall was gone, and then we came out of the bathroom together. Stella and Gloria went to their math class, and I went to English. We were reading *Adam Bede*. It was so boring that the teacher was having us read it aloud in class just to make sure that we read at least part of it. The Big Four ignored me when I came in, and I ignored them, too. But I knew that whatever was going on with them wasn't over and that it was going to include Gloria, me, and Brian, because we were on Stella's side and they were the other side. That was the way things worked in seventh grade.

Gloria called me that night. I was allowed to talk to my friends for ten minutes, and I had to do it in the living room or the kitchen, because that's where the phones were, so I couldn't really ask questions. What I learned was that Stella got in trouble with her mom and was grounded for a week for "sneaky behavior," that she couldn't talk to Brian for more than ten minutes anymore, and that she had had to go to the principal's office for calling Mary A. a bad name right out in the hall by the front door. What made her mom extra mad was that while she was in the principal's office, the bus left without her, and her mother had to come pick her up. And she had left her book bag in her locker, so she couldn't even do her homework. Gloria said she felt sorry for Stella since, "Nothing was her fault to start out with," and I said that I felt sorry for Stella, too. After I hung up, Daddy said, "What's that all about?"

"Nothing, really."

"Must be something."

I shrugged.

He stared at me. I idled around the living room for a minute, then went up to my room. Once upon a time, I would have told him all about it, just because it wasn't me who was in trouble, and it was all pretty interesting. But I knew what he would say: "Pride goeth before destruction, and a haughty spirit before a fall." I didn't think it was as easy as that.

In and Out Jump

Jump with Branches

Coop Jump

Chapter 9

WITH ALL THE NEW HORSES, IT WASN'T HARD TO LEAVE ORNERY George alone. And March was a busy month. First, Daddy sold Jewel Number 1 as a ranch horse, which was a nice enough life for her. She was good with the cows and never afraid of them. She could get by on hay and no grain, so they liked her for that. And later we learned that one day, she was out on the ranch with the owner, an old man, looking for a stray calf. He asked the Jewel (they kept her name, Jewel) to cross a dry riverbed, and she refused. Even though he hit her with the quirt and spurred her, she balked. Well, by that time, the owner was pretty mad, but he got off and went around to lead her to show her there was no problem with the river, except that there was—it was quicksand, and he sank up to his knees before she pulled him out by backing away while he held on to the reins. After that, of course, she had a home for life and a friend for life. We heard this story because the man called Daddy up and told him, and thanked him for selling him "a brainy one," and all things considered, well, she had been cheap at the price. When he was telling us about this over dinner, Daddy said, "I never would have known she had that in her, but who can tell? Thank you, Lord."

"Amen," said Mom.

The chestnut George got sold as a trail horse to a big hotel, and Daddy said that he might live a long time. When all a horse did all day was walk along at an easy pace, he could live to be thirty or more. And, of course, since he was at a big hotel, in a fancy barn right beside the golf course, they would keep him clean and shiny. In the summer, they were going to put him in a camp for little kids. So, all in all, Daddy was happy in spite of Ornery George and the death of the mare. Other years had been worse, and I knew not to ask about them.

The new horses were in full work now. Daddy and I rode horses until sundown every night and fed after dark. Jack was eating hay now, but he still had to be fed his milk, with bran mixed into it, in a bucket, several times a day, which was time-consuming. Mom was good with the horses because she was good with all animals, including baby birds and lost dogs, but she didn't ride unless she was going on the trail and the horse was old and quiet. I made myself extra work, rubbing Jack with the chamois so that he would always be happy to see me. In other words, we were busy, but when Miss Slater called and said the horse show was coming up and could I come and ride in a few classes, it seemed as easy as you please to get out my English riding clothes and brush them off, then shine up my jodphur boots and drive over there. I had never shown in them before, but Daddy had gotten them secondhand somewhere and had always told me they would come in handy. Daddy picked me up after school. The truck was clean, too, and Daddy was wearing his good hat.

I was to ride that afternoon, just to get the feel of the pony again, and then the next morning, Saturday, I was to take him in three classes—pony hunter over fences, two feet; pony hunter over fences, two feet, six inches; and pony hunter hack (no jumps). This time, Miss Slater said, Melinda would watch and learn. Maybe next time she would try it herself.

When I got there, Melinda was nowhere to be seen, and when Miss Slater saw me looking around for her, she said, "Poor Melinda. She's home with a tummy ache. I'm sure it's not serious."

I said, "Does she ride the pony much?"

"You mean Gallant Man, here?"

"Is that what you named him, Gallant Man?"

Miss Slater smiled. She said, "The original Gallant Man was a racehorse some years ago. He was quite small. When my dad took me to the Belmont Stakes that year, he put a bet on him for me, even though he himself preferred another horse. Gallant Man won, and in record time. So when I saw what a nice pony we had here and how he is ready to do anything we ask of him, I thought it would be a cute name for him. What did you call him?"

"We called him George. But that's what we call all of them."

"So you won't get attached."

I nodded.

She didn't say anything about Melinda. I then mounted the pony. He was completely accustomed to the stable now, so he was as calm as he ever was at home, though there were flags flapping and horses and riders and grooms and trainers everywhere, and tents, too. Riders were showing in the main ring, in front of the biggest tent, and in another ring behind the tent. Miss Slater led me to a smaller ring that was fairly distant from all the brouhaha, down toward the trees. Daddy waved us off and went into the stands to watch the action.

Eight jumps were set out in the ring, and we had it to ourselves. The jumps were a fair selection, with colorful striped poles, flowers in boxes, and branches arranged like hedges. There were two chicken coops and two gates, too. The pony didn't look at anything. He had seen it all in the month or so since coming here.

Miss Slater had me walk, trot, and canter both directions, with a few small circles, some halts, some shortened strides, and some lengthened strides. After that she had me warm up over some crossbars and some plain poles, the way we would warm up for a show round the next morning. Finally, she called me to the center of the ring and gave me a course. It was simple enough—I was to go to the right, jumping the white gate, then the red and white poles. After that, I was to cut across the ring diagonally, jumping one of the coops. Then I was to make a short left turn, take the blue and white poles at the end of the ring, then the one-stride in-and-out on the far side, finishing up over the black and white gate. The last exercise was to turn the pony in one nice circle on the proper lead and come down quietly to the trot and the walk.

It wasn't as easy as it looked.

I can't say that Daddy and I ever thought in terms of "courses" of jumps. For one thing, we didn't have very many standards or poles and for another, we weren't in the jumping horse business. That was probably why I lost my way after the third jump, turned right instead of left, and was faced with the first jump again, even though I knew that was wrong. We jumped it and then I pulled Gallant Man to a halt. Miss Slater came over. "Mixed up?"

"Yes, ma'am."

"Okay, try this." She had me just go around the outside of the arena, jumping each of the seven jumps as they were set, including the in-and-out, which was two fences set one stride apart. You jumped twice, but it counted, for scoring purposes, as one effort. This, too, was harder than it looked, but I made it. When I came back to her, she said, "Abby, that wasn't bad."

I knew there was a *but* coming.

"But you seemed a little out of control. This time, I want you to go more slowly, sit up more in the turns, and not let the pony lean to the inside."

When I did it again, I realized how bad the previous time had been by the fact that I actually felt the pony canter to the jumps this time in a balanced way and jump them in a balanced way, without leaning to the inside. The last thing you want your pony to do when he's jumping is take them tilted.

She said, "I would like you to think about the jumps that

are coming up when you are going *into* the corner of the arena rather than coming out of it."

I tried this the third time around. It was much better.

This time she said, "You're a fast learner. And a good rider. Try the first course again."

She stood with me in the center of the ring and gestured to demonstrate the course again. I was to fix the turns in my mind first and the jumps in my mind second.

I repeated the course back to her.

She said, "That's right. One other thing."

"What?"

"Look where you are going to be ten strides ahead, not two or five strides ahead."

It was easy.

In fact, that night in bed, I lay there for a fairly long time, trying to figure out how it had gone so quickly from being impossible the first time to being easy the last time. I pictured the jumps in my mind, one after another. I realized that the most important thing was not that I was jumping jumps, but that I was riding a route from one spot to another, just like on a map. If I remembered the map and sat up, we would get there.

When we arrived at the show the next morning, Daddy went right up to Melinda's father, Mr. Frederick Anniston, held out his hand, and introduced himself. Mr. Anniston was wearing a tweed jacket and another coat and a dark-colored hat with a green feather in the band. He had on gloves and seemed to be cold; Melinda was pressed against him and looked as though the weather had shrunk her down to nothing. Melinda's mother didn't seem to be around. Mr. Anniston didn't speak to me, but he watched me.

There were six other ponies in the warm-up area, which was fairly large, and six trainers calling out to six riders. Two of the ponies were very fancy—they almost looked more like reduced-size horses than ponies. The other four were just ponies. Gallant Man, the only gray, was prettier than all of those four. I wove my way among the other ponies—this part wasn't hard. After we warmed up, Daddy held Gallant Man, and Miss Slater walked with me around the course, step by step, so that I could learn it on my feet. The course had more than two turns—it had four—and more than seven fences. If you counted both halves of the in-and-out, it had nine fences.

I got back on Gallant Man. One of the girls and her pony were jumping the jumps in the warm-up area, a crossbar, a single bar, and an oxer, which was two bars parallel to one another, the back one a little higher than the front one. Her pony was one of the plain ones. He was willing, but he looked dull to me. The girl counted as she approached every fence—"One two one two one two one two"—and then they jumped. The other thing she did was lift her eyes higher and higher as she got closer to the fence, so that when she was over the top, she was looking up into the trees. This made me smile.

We warmed up by trotting the cross-rail, then cantering it. He kept me right with him, and by the time we were ready for a real jump, I couldn't wait. But I did. One thing I knew (and there weren't many of those) was to wait. I took slow breaths. I could see Mr. Anniston standing by the rail, staring at us. Melinda was pressed up against his leg. Neither one was smiling.

Now we did the oxer—first small, then bigger, then big. I did my best to think, Slow. Level. Slow. Level.

Then they called my number and Miss Slater walked me to the gate into the arena. I stood there until the previous pony came out. The jumps looked like an absolute jumble. They were all plain, natural brown or white, no colors. That made it worse. I walked and then trotted the pony to the other end of the ring, and then, completely panicked, I asked him to start his canter circle. I wasn't panicked about the jumping—the jumps were small. I was panicked about the feeling that I was in a sea of jumps and had no idea how to make my way around it. But I did know where the first jump was and the second. After that, I saw the third, which was a white chicken coop, and then it was one jump after the other, and all too soon, we were done and doing our final canter circle. The trot. And then we walked out of the ring. I was filled up with the thrill of the whole thing, the cantering, the turning, the jumping. I could have gone around all day.

Miss Slater met me at the gate. She said, "That was fine, Abby, for a first round. Next time, just a degree slower. Do you have a rhythm? Think the same rhythm, but slow it down." She glanced over toward Mr. Anniston. He still wasn't smiling, but he nodded. In the meantime, Daddy trotted over to us now that we were back in the warm-up area, and he kissed me on the cheek. When I took off my hard hat, he ruffled my hair. I was really glad he was my daddy rather than Mr. Anniston.

I walked the pony around, and Daddy walked with us. He was saying, "This is fun here. This isn't bad at all. You know Black George? He could do this. Most of these horses look just like him but don't have as pretty a head. Yes, this gives me an idea. Yes, yes, it does." Then he went off and got me a hot dog, and I ate it sitting on the fence, holding the pony. Daddy had a lump of sugar for him, which we sneaked to him when Miss Slater wasn't looking. I didn't know for sure that she was against treats, but I suspect she would be that type, as she was very neat.

We got a ribbon in the class—fifth place out of ten ponies. I took it over to Melinda and gave it to her, and she smiled and said thank you, but she held it limply in her hand, like she was going to drop it any second. I guess I had never really seen anyone like Melinda before. She was scared of her own shadow.

The sun came out in time for the second class, which was a hack class, no jumping. All we had to do was walk, trot, canter, turn around, trot again, halt, canter again, according to the commands that the judge called out. A fancy pony who wasn't very nice pinned his ears and bucked once while the judge was looking right at him. Some of the other ponies had trouble with their leads. However, Gallant Man was easy and perfect, and he won the blue ribbon.

Afterward, Daddy said, "You know, I've been walking around, pretending I'd like to buy one of these horses, a show horse like these—not necessarily a pony, because a good pony is just luck—anyway, some of these horses cost ten thousand dollars. All of them five to ten." He was grinning.

Now it was past noon and time for the third class. I thought it was silly that the first class and the second class were equal, with the second class being so easy, but it was true, and the pony was in contention for a champion award. The course for the third class was almost like the first course but with one less turn and higher jumps. Miss Slater and I walked it. Melinda went with us, leaving Mr. Anniston standing by the fence.

We walked from jump to jump, right from the back middle of every fence to the front middle of the next fence, Miss Slater taking steady even steps. She said to me, "This is your path, Abby. Think of it as a red line going around the course. You just stay on the red line and slow your rhythm a little bit and look right between that pony's ears all the time, okay?"

"Okay."

Then Melinda took my hand for a moment. The first thing she said all day was, "He's my pony."

I said, "I know that, Melinda. I'm not taking him back."

"But if he's not good enough, Papa will sell him and get another one."

I realized what she meant. I said, "How many chances does he get, Melinda?"

Melinda looked up at me. "I don't know. Not many. I'm scared of another pony."

Miss Slater glanced at me. She said, "Well, let's not think about all of that now. He's a good pony. Do you understand the course, Abby?"

I nodded. I understood the course and everything else, to tell the truth. My own opinion was that even if Melinda just wanted the pony to stand around and eat carrots, that's what she should have. I went back to the barn, and the groom brought out Gallant Man. I mounted at the mounting block and went into the warm-up. The whole time, it was like the eyes of Mr. Anniston were freezing a hole in my back. It made me mad. It made me sit up and lift my chin. I knew that Miss Slater liked the pony a lot, and if something happened, she would find the pony another home. I knew also that it wasn't my worry or Daddy's, but anyway. I sat up. I made myself float around the warm-up as if the other ponies were not worth looking at.

The bell rang. I heard my name. I passed the previous pony in the gate. We trotted to the end of the ring and did our circle.

This time, the jumps were higher, and so they were more fun. I could feel the pony curling underneath me, rising under me and then landing and cantering on. The jumps, the very centers of the jumps, came up one by one right between the pony's ears, right between my ears, too. The other thing that the pony had to do correctly in order to win, which was change leads in the turns, he did perfectly well. He was automatic at that and it didn't worry me. It was the pace and the style that would tell the tale. We came over the last jump. I asked the pony for his circle, then for the trot, then for the walk. I dropped the rein contact and lifted my chin. As we exited the ring, I took a deep breath, as if I were Mary A. or one of those other girls at school, ignoring everyone who didn't make any difference. I pretended to be Mary A. all the way back to the barn. Miss Slater and Daddy clapped for us.

The pony came second, after a blond fellow, whose round I didn't see. We got reserve champion. Since it was the pony who was being judged, not the rider, Melinda went into the ring, leading Gallant Man, wearing her best riding clothes. They gave her a long red and yellow ribbon and a silver dish for mints. She came out smiling and hugged me. I glanced over at Mr. Anniston. At last he was smiling, even though it was a small, only semi-happy smile. It got bigger when Melinda ran over to him. He picked her up and gave her a kiss on the cheek, but it all looked fake to me—not as if he didn't love her and wasn't happy for her, but as if he had lots of ideas and keeping the pony was only one of them. I saw his eyes follow the blond pony, who had won champion. But nobody knew those people, and Miss Slater said they were from down south. As we were untacking the pony, she said, "You can't believe what horses cost down there. It's a crime. It really is."

On the way home from the show, I reported this to Daddy. He said, "Is that so? Is that so, indeed?" When we got home, he pulled Black George out of the paddock and had me stand him up so that his feet were square and his head was up, ears pricked. Then he walked around him, peering at him. After a few minutes, he said to me, "Now, Abby, look how he stands. His back legs are set right under his haunches and his front legs are set just a hair behind the straight, but his knees are a smidgen bent. That's called being 'over at the knee,' and it's not a bad thing. His croup has a nice slope, and his neck comes up out of his withers. And his throatlatch, where his head is attached to his neck, that has a nice curve to it. The Lord himself only knows what he was doing for a living in Oklahoma, given how bad his feet were and what a job it was to do his teeth, but I know what he's gonna do for a living, so your job tonight is to write down everything Miss Slater said to you, and then we'll read it over together and see if we can learn something."

My paper had seven things on it. Daddy read it over a couple of times and said, "This is a nice puzzle. I think we're going to have a good time."

Seven things:

1. Ride the course, not the jumps.
2. Keep the horse level, especially through the corners.
3. Look ahead ten strides, not two or five.
4. Ride to the middle of every fence.
5. Wait.
6. Maintain a rhythm.
7. Look up, never down.

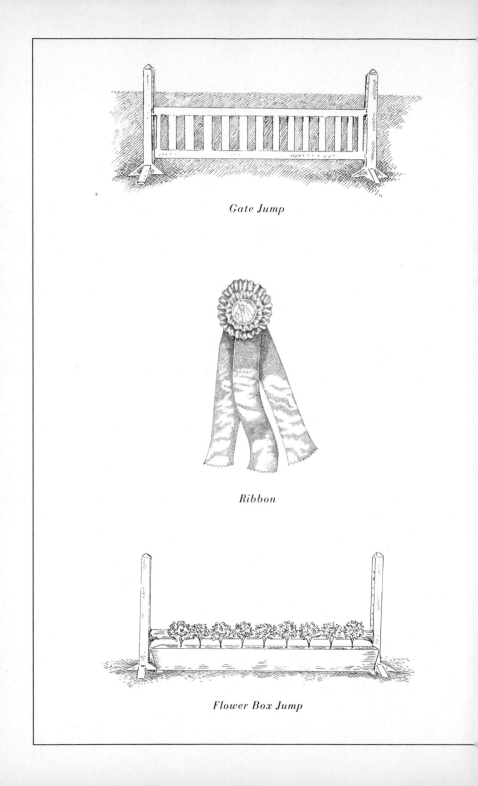

Gate Jump

Ribbon

Flower Box Jump

Chapter 10

SOMETIMES A LUCKY THING HAPPENS, AND FOR US IT WAS THAT Mr. Tacker, the old man who had Jewel, decided he needed two more ranch horses, so he came by to look at what we had. Of course we had Black George and Ornery George. The other George was a chestnut with two white socks in front, so we called him Socks George. We also had the mares. The old man bought Red Jewel right off the bat—she was well broke and, now that she'd been with us for a month, neatly shod and a deal fatter than she had been. He didn't want any of the others, but he looked twice at Ornery George. Then he looked again. He said to Daddy, but glancing at me, "Your girl ride this one?"

Daddy said, "She has been. What with the new shipment,

111

we've given him a bit of a rest. . . ." He shrugged. Not exactly bearing false witness.

"Well built."

"He is a stylish one," said Daddy. "Looks like a reining horse, if you ask me."

"Has he been around cattle?"

"Supposed to have been, back in Oklahoma. I can't guarantee . . ."

"What would you say to a tryout?"

"I don't know about that. I'll have to think about that."

Now, the fact was, Daddy didn't mind a tryout. As he said, his horses had nothing to hide, and generally they were just the same if they went away for a week as they were at home. But then, that very thing would be the problem with Ornery George.

Daddy stuck his hands in his pockets. He said, "Mr. Tacker, I don't want to say no, but I can't really say yes at this point." He gestured toward Red Jewel, who was standing quietly with her head down. I stepped over to her and scratched her beneath her ear. She cocked a hind foot. Very relaxed. He said, "I think you're gonna like this mare. She's a useful animal."

But he could see the light in Mr. Tacker's eyes, and so could I. I knew that when he was taking off his boots to go to bed that night, he would have a picture of Ornery George in his mind, not one of the very useful and sedate Red Jewel. I said, "What are you going to name the mare?" I said this in that bright way you say things when you are trying to distract the grown-ups from what they are thinking.

Mr. Tacker looked down at me. He said, "What's her name, Red Jewel?"

I nodded.

"Well, that looks to me like 'Ruby.' I'm sure she'll do fine."
And he led her off toward his trailer. Of course, he looked back
at Ornery George two or three times before he got her into the
trailer and drove away. He paid eight hundred dollars for her.
What with the shipping from Oklahoma, two shoeings, and
the teeth, Daddy had about four hundred into her, so he was
happy at supper. He said, "He wants to come back next week,
but I put him off. And then he's going out of town for a week,
up to a cattle show. So that's maybe two and a half weeks we've
got to figure something out."

Mom set down the early peas, put her hands on her hips,
and said, "Figure what out?"

"How to get that horse right so he can ride him. Those two
mares—"

I interrupted, "Jewel and Ruby!"

"—are fine for him, because even though he's old and a little
stiff, he used to be good on a horse. And he still thinks he is."

Mom shook her head and then shook it again. "Mark," she
said, "that's a dangerous game."

"It was him who noticed the horse and asked me about
him. I had to answer his questions, didn't I? I couldn't be un-
friendly about the horse. That makes people suspicious."

But we all knew that wasn't the right response. And I knew
Daddy would have me up on Ornery George sooner or later, most
likely sooner, and what he would say about it was, "Let's just give
it a try and see what happens," and I would know what was going
to happen perfectly well, and it wouldn't be good. The funny
thing was that I could ride all the others without any problems
and I had gone to the horse show and done something new without worrying, but I couldn't stop fretting about Ornery George.

Mr. Tacker had come by on a Thursday. On Friday, Brian Connelly ate lunch with Mary A. and Joan. Five minutes after he sat down, Stella got up, took her tray to the trash area, and dumped everything, including the plate, into the trash bin. Then she walked out. Gloria put her hand on my knee and muttered, "We should listen in and tell her everything they say," so we did.

Brian talked about his lunch. He opened his brown paper sack and took out everything and lined it up on the table. He had a peanut butter and bacon sandwich on white bread, a navel orange, six carrot sticks, a gingersnap, a napkin, and a carton of milk. His lunch, according to him, was full of protein and vitamins (especially vitamins A and C). A gingersnap was the only really nutritious cookie there is. The two girls didn't say anything, and I secretly watched Mary A. and Joan while he was explaining this. They kept exchanging glances, which included some raised eyebrows, but when they finished with their lunches, they waited for him. As they passed our table on the way out, Joan said, "Oh, hi, Gloria. Is Stella sick or something?"

Gloria shrugged. Joan and Mary A. both gave me big show-off smiles and then they frog-marched Brian out of the lunchroom and down the hall. When they were really gone, we jumped up, got rid of our trays, and ran to look for Stella. We found her in the bathroom, of course. Gloria started in. "You can't believe what they talked about."

"He described his whole lunch to them, and it was sitting right there on the table in front of them."

"He told them about the difference between plant protein and animal protein."

"He said he didn't have quite enough B vitamins, but he would have more at dinner."

"It took him about an hour to peel his orange. He had to peel the whole thing in one piece."

But it didn't work, because she started crying. The bell rang, and we went to class, leaving her there. I guess sometime after that, her mom came and picked her up, and she was counted absent for the rest of the afternoon. The Big Four paid no attention to me, but they were loud, and Joan and Mary N. got sent to the principal's office for passing notes. By the end of the day, I was tired of school all over again.

I can't say I'd planned to defy the righteous authority of my father. Although I had refused to ride Ornery George before, I wasn't all that clear in my own mind whether my refusal still stood. I rode Blue Jewel and Black George with no problems, one in my western saddle and one in my English saddle. We weren't yet jumping Black George, but I was trying to make him go around the way the pony had in the hack class, even and smooth, going into the corners and never leaning to the inside. I practiced holding a rein in each hand, bending my elbows, thumbs up, heels down, back straight, body square.

When I got off Black George, I saw that Daddy had Ornery George tied up and groomed and my western saddle on him, all cinched up and ready to go. Ornery George looked at me out of the corner of his eye, but he didn't turn his head. I put my hand on the stirrup, and he switched his tail. Daddy was bent under him, picking his foot and talking. "He's not a bad fellow. Willful, a bit, but not actually unkind. You'll do . . ." Daddy let the foot drop, and George shifted his weight toward me. This was another sign, him pushing his haunch at me. I could read these signs just as easily as another horse might—they meant, I'm the boss. They also meant, as far was I was concerned, that he was ready, and even eager, to show me a thing or two. That was the difference between the old George and the new George—with the old George, you had to go and find the resentment, but with the new George, he had it out ready to show you.

I said, "He seems a little grumpy."

"You can work him out of that."

"If he's going to a man, you should work him out of it yourself."

Daddy stood up and looked at me, frowning, I'm sure, at my "tone," but all he said was, "Could be. But if I get on him, we might end up going down the trail that your uncle Luke blazed for me. I don't want to go down that trail. He needs to return to where he was with you."

I wiped my mouth with the back of my hand, because I knew I was about to say something more sassy. I said, "Where he was with me was that I refused to ride him."

Daddy threw the hoof pick into the brush box and blew out his lips. Then he said, "Flat refusal?"

"Well, I—"

"Defiant refusal? Defiant refusal to even try?"

"Look at him!"

"What's wrong with him? He's just standing here."

"He was switching his tail. He—"

"He what?"

"He gave me a look."

"You defiantly refuse to get on him because he gave you a look?"

"I don't . . ."

"Yes or no?"

"Yes, I refuse, or no, I won't ride him?" If I was going to get in trouble, I wanted to be sure that we both agreed on what I was getting in trouble for.

"Listen, miss—"

"No, I won't ride him. I don't want to get bucked off again and I don't trust him." Rather than look at Daddy's face, I turned away, picked up a halter and lead rope, and went to get Socks George. When I returned, Daddy had put Ornery George in the pasture. He helped me with Socks George, and we finished for the day after dark, as usual. He was very polite at dinner, the way he could be when he had given up on you and turned you over to the Lord. After dinner, I did the safest thing and went into my room and did my homework, as I always did on Friday night, because I wasn't allowed to do homework on Sunday, and Saturday night I was often too tired. I knew Daddy was giving me more leeway than he had ever given Danny, but even thinking that made me so nervous that I just kept reading *Adam Bede* until I lost the thread of the story completely and fell asleep. Mom came in late to help me out of my clothes and into bed. If I hadn't been so groggy, I would have talked to her, because even though she never went against him, she sometimes told me how he worked.

The next day was Saturday, and Daddy was already up and the hay was already delivered to the horses, and he was already gone by the time I opened my eyes. I found out the reason during breakfast—the shoer, Jake Morrisson, was pulling through the gate in his truck, and my brother, Danny, was with him. Mom popped up and ran out the door, and when the truck stopped, Danny jumped out and gave her a big hug. I swallowed the last of my toast and hurried out, too. Usually Jake came during the week, when I was at school. This time, he'd been busy all week, and Saturday was his only spot. It had been six weeks since all the new horses had been shod, so here they were. Danny grabbed my shoulders and kissed me on the forehead, and Mom put a wrapped package into the passenger side of the shoeing truck. All of this reminded me that what had happened with Danny—six months, now—was really bad, and even though we acted like everything was okay, it wasn't. While Mr. Morrisson was setting up his anvil and his forge and all, Mom took Danny aside and looked at him and asked him questions, but I didn't hear what she asked or what he answered. When things were set up, he gave her another hug and came back over to put on his apron.

He said, "I heard you showed those society girls a thing or two with that pony a week ago, missy."

"Only a thing. Not two."

He laughed.

"It was fun. But now there's work to be done."

"I'm sure there is."

Before, I had come up to his chin. Now I came up to his shoulder. And his shoulders were big, too, no doubt from learning to shoe horses. In his leather apron, he looked bowlegged and grown up. Jake Morrisson said, "Who's first?"

We got through Blue Jewel and Socks George. They behaved themselves and were reset all around.

Ornery George, however, needed new shoes. I went and got him while Danny stoked up the fire and Jake looked in his shoe stock for the right size to begin with.

118

Out in the gelding corral, Ornery George could see me coming, and no doubt he could put two and two together—the shoeing truck was here, two horses had come and gone already, and he was next. Therefore, he went around behind the other horses, and when I passed through them and tried to catch him, he threw up his head and trotted away. I walked after him. Normally, I didn't have this problem, but there was plenty of hay in the corral, he had eaten his fill, and the only thing I meant to him was taking time out from his day to do yet another thing that humans demanded of him. He trotted off again and again every time I got anywhere near him.

Finally, Danny called from the gate, "What's wrong with this one?"

"At the moment, he doesn't want to be caught. Normally, plenty else, too. He wasn't very nice, and then Uncle Luke got on him and . . ."

"And that was that!" Danny laughed and pulled the gate latch backward. He came in, closed the gate after himself, and held out his hand for the halter and lead rope. I said, "With pleasure."

But Danny didn't head for the horse. He walked along the fence with his head down and his arms by his sides, and after a few steps, several of the horses were looking at him. Then he turned toward Ornery George, and when Ornery George looked at him, he waved the halter and lead rope so that Ornery George backed up and then trotted off. After that, he walked toward George, still making him trot away. Then he put his arms down and turned left again, into the group of other horses. At the far end of the corral, George had stopped and was looking at him. Now Danny turned right and walked along the fence, not toward Ornery George or away from him. When he saw George was looking toward him, he waved him off again, and George turned, tossed his head, and trotted away. But he looked back.

Now Danny seemed to ignore George, and George walked toward him. When Danny stopped among the other three, George was looking as hard as he could, possibly wondering why the other three were so interested in Danny. When George approached the others, Danny let him get fairly close, then he waved him off and walked toward the gate. The others followed, and George followed them. Pretty soon, he was standing at the gate with the other three. Danny didn't do a thing that showed he cared. He just walked down the line of horses, giving each of them a word and a pat, same with Ornery George, nothing special. Then he patted each one in turn again, but when he got to Ornery George, he slipped the lead rope around his neck. Then he stroked his neck for a long time, then he traced figure eights around his eyes. He eased the halter on. It seemed as though Danny was in no hurry at all.

Pretty soon, Danny walked briskly out into the middle of the corral, the lead rope in his right hand and Ornery George following behind. When they got into the center, Danny walked him in a couple of circles, then sent him in a circle in each direction. When the horse was finished doing this, Danny turned abruptly and walked back toward the gate. George followed. He looked a little confused, or maybe that's not the word. Just not quite sure of what was going on and why. I opened the gate. Danny and George walked right past me and over to Jake Morrisson. He stood up for the shoer and gave no problems. When Danny put him back in the corral, he led him through the other horses and out to the middle. There he sent him in a circle in each direction again, then he had him turn and come to him. He waited. Ornery George looked around, his head up and his ears pricked. Danny just stood there. It wasn't until George lowered his head that Danny took the halter off, and when he did, he sent the horse away rather than letting him trot away on his own.

When Danny met me at the gate, I said, "You've got to come back."

"Why is that, sis?"

"Because that horse is going to kill me."

Danny laughed. "No, he's not."

"Yes, he is, because Daddy has made up his mind that I'm going to ride him, and every time I do, he tries to buck me off. And he's a good and dedicated bucker."

"Don't ride him."

"He's been here almost six months. He's got to get sold."

Danny knew about the six-months rule. The six-months rule was that after a horse had been here for six months, even talking about him made Daddy mad.

"I've never seen you be afraid of a horse before."

"You always rode the hard ones. You know what he says— how can I—"

"Say that a kid can ride this horse if you can't ride it?"

"A little girl. That's what he says now."

"What did Uncle Luke do with the horse?"

"Laid him down."

"With the rope?"

I nodded.

"Sat on his shoulder?"

"And sang four verses of 'Stewball.'"

"'I bet on the gray mare, I bet on the bay, if I'da bet on old Stewball—'"

Listening to Danny sing made me miss him like crazy, but I just chimed in, "'I'd be a free man today.'" Then I said, "Yeah. That one."

Danny ruffled my hair. "When do you have to ride him again?"

I shrugged. We walked the horse out of the pasture. Every time I had seen Danny since he left—this was the fourth time—I knew just by looking at him that he wasn't going to pay the price he'd have to pay to come back. Daddy and Danny and everyone we knew could deplore pride and a haughty spirit until they were blue in the face, but that didn't make either pride or a haughty spirit go away.

Jake Morrisson was finishing up on the last horse, the third mare. Danny now helped him put all his things away, and pretty soon, they were loaded up. But I didn't think Mom was going to leave it at that, and of course she came out of the kitchen, wiping her hands, and invited the two of them to stay for lunch—she had some brisket and homemade bread and, amazingly enough, she had just baked a lemon meringue pie! Danny's favorite, imagine that, so we went in and everyone washed up, and we all had lunch, but Mom didn't really eat. She just sat in her place at the end of the table, with Danny catty-corner from her, and she talked and joked while we ate and asked Jake Morrisson if Danny was doing a good job, and Jake said he was, he was especially good with the horses, and someday he would figure out what the business end of a hammer was, Mr. Morrisson was sure of that. We all laughed.

While Mom and Mr. Morrisson drank cups of coffee, I took Danny out to Jack's corral to have a look at him.

Jack was over two months old now and big and strong. Normally, he trotted right over to me as soon as he saw me, but now we could see him over in the far corner of the corral, with his nose down and his ears pricked. Though there was some fresh grass in the pen, he wasn't eating it. I said, "What's he doing?"

"He's watching something."

He seemed transfixed, so we crept around the outside of the corral, quietly but not sneakily, since we didn't want to startle him, but nor did we want to distract him. Whatever he was watching moved, and Jack took a step to follow it, then he pushed his nose down farther and sniffed. By this time we were close to the corner, and Danny squatted down and peered through the wire mesh. Then he laughed. "He's watching a gecko."

The gecko must have run off at that point, because Jack snorted, threw up his head, and leapt into the air. Once he did that, he put his nose down again, right where the gecko had been, but finding nothing, he flicked his ears and walked over to the fence. When he got to me, he stuck out his nose. I said, "The other day, he followed a stray cat all over the corral, that orange cat with one ear."

"That big tom," said Danny.

"Jack would follow him, sniffing at him. The cat wasn't scared at all. At one point, the cat was lying there and Jack reached his nose down and the cat suddenly sat up and batted him. Jack just jumped. It was so funny."

We stroked the side of his face for a bit, where the foal hair had begun to be replaced by the silky dark coat the color of black walnut that would be his adult color. He had no white on him, except for four white hairs in the middle of his forehead. I put my hand on his neck, and he stretched over the fence. I started stroking him firmly along the length of his neck, the way I did with the chamois. Air ruffled in his nostrils.

"He's going to be a nice horse," said Danny, fingering Jack's sparse little black mane.

"I love him."

"Mom told me what happened to the mare."

I didn't say anything.

"Ab, you know that orphan foals rarely come to much and can be very dangerous."

"No, I didn't know that." I kept stroking.

"Who's going to push this little guy around, the way his dam would?"

"I don't know."

He took his hat off and waved it in Jack's face. Jack jumped back and trotted off a few steps, his tail high. Then he tipped forward, kicked out twice, and took off across the corral, giving two or three high-pitched whinnies. He bucked a couple of times. When he came to the fence on the far side, he executed a sharp left turn and galloped five strides before dropping back to the trot. Then he trotted toward us, his ears pricked and his nostrils wide. He was snorting, looking for the hat, which Danny had put back on his head. Now came the funny part— when he got back to where we were standing by the fence, he stuck his nose out and sniffed Danny's hat. Danny obligingly cocked his head forward so that Jack could sniff to his heart's content. When he was done, he gave a big sigh and his ears went floppy again. I started stroking his neck. Danny said, "Did you see how quick and self-confident he is? He needs someone to be telling him what to do, and it isn't going to be you."

"You don't know how he is. He's really sweet."

"I'm just saying, don't count on anything."

"Well, now you do sound like Daddy."

A scowl, but only a little one. He fixed his expression almost immediately and said, "Maybe so, but I'm just saying."

"I heard you."

I felt grumpy as we walked around the barn, but then Danny said, "I don't know what the mare looked like, but he's a Thoroughbred for sure. Abby, he's a beautiful colt. And he's going to be a beautiful horse." He glanced at me. "But don't get your hopes up."

I don't know what Jake Morrisson and Mom were talking about all this time, but I'm sure it was plenty, since not only did Danny work for Jake, he also lived above his barn, where his ranch hands had once lived when he still had the whole ranch. But they sorted everything out, and Jake called us over. Danny got in the truck, everybody waved, and they drove off. Afterward, Mom seemed happy enough. All she said to me, though, was, "No evidence that he's doing anything stupid."

I said, "That's good."

"He bought his own car."

"Well, I'm sure he did. What kind?"

"Fifty-six Chevy convertible."

This made us both laugh, but then Mom said, "I think a convertible would be fun, even if it is almost ten years old. We can get him to take us for a drive."

Tack Box

Farrier's Tools

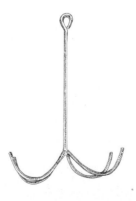

Tack Cleaning Hook

Chapter 11

THERE WAS NO RIDING, THANK YOU, LORD, ON SUNDAY, AND MY favorite cook, Miss Larrabee, brought supper to church. We had chicken with dumplings, homemade bread, and because she and her brother were avid gardeners plenty of homegrown asparagus with a sauce made from their homegrown lemons. The Larrabees swore by rotted horse manure as a fertilizer, so they came by our place several times a year and carted off part of the manure pile. Over supper, they said that their strawberries looked better this year than they ever had, and everybody at the table kind of sighed at the thought of the strawberry shortcake to come.

There were two different theories about shortcake in our church—Mom and Daddy and some of the others preferred something like a sweetened biscuit, crumbly and crisp on the bottom, split and filled with strawberries and whipped cream. Miss Larrabee and her brother and some of their side preferred a dense, sweet pound cake shaped like a crown, with the center of the crown filled with berries and topped with ice cream. All of the kids liked both kinds equally, and we looked forward to the first strawberries of the year, which made a sort of celebration of our church. I won't say that Daddy and all of the others agreed about everything they thought and talked about, but I will say they never argued about the strawberries.

Eating the chicken and dumplings and thinking about the strawberry shortcakes to come reminded me that things at church had been very peaceful lately—even the Greeley children were willing to sit quietly three out of every ten minutes, or however long it took to read one picture book. The one they liked best was *The Little Engine That Could*, which had nothing enlightening in it about the Lord, but it was the one that kept them quiet, so that was the one Carlie and I read to them, over and over, six times apiece on that Sunday alone.

And then Monday and Tuesday, it poured rain, so I kept Daddy happy by cleaning and oiling all the tack. On Wednesday, the arena was soaking wet, and Thursday, Daddy had to go into town for the entire day, not my fault. When we finally got to ride on Friday, we had to do all the easy horses first, and by that time, it was dark.

On Saturday, it was sunny as you please. The footing in the arena was perfect, and I was sitting over my French toast, dreading the morning. In my mind, Ornery George had gobbled up all the others, and I dreaded riding him so much that I didn't look forward even to Black George, who was turning out to be quite nice. It was seven a.m.; we were getting a bright and early start, and just as Daddy pushed his chair back to stand up, there was a knock at the back door.

"Who could that be, I wonder," said Mom. But she said it in a funny way, as if she didn't wonder at all.

The man at the door took off his hat as soon as she opened it. They spoke for a moment or two, and then she brought him in, with a smile. He wasn't a very big man, what Daddy would call wiry rather than rangy, and he had on faded brown pants and very old boots, with a blue denim shirt and leather vest. He said that he was pleased to meet us. Daddy shook his hand, because you never knew if someone came to your door whether it was Jesus or not, and in fact there was a Greek myth about this very same thing. The man said his name was James Jarrow, called Jem, and he had heard from Jake Morrisson that we had some nice horses for sale.

"We do, indeed," said Daddy, and he got his business face on, which was simultaneously friendly and efficient. He said, "Let's go look, shall we?"

Mom said, "Abby has finished her breakfast. She can go along," which was the first clue that she had something up her sleeve. However, I put on my jacket and my boots and followed the two men out to the corrals. The horses were eating their hay. Jack was eating hay, too, even though we were still giving him some milk, usually mixed with bran. I had already fed him that, and he had licked the bucket clean.

Jem Jarrow was not a talkative person. He went with Daddy to each corral, stood by the gate, and stared at the horses. He didn't fidget in any way. Next to him, Daddy looked like a jack-in-the-box, jumping up and down and making noise, but Daddy was just normal. It was Jem Jarrow who was different.

It must have taken him twenty minutes to stare at all the horses, including Jack. Finally, he went back to the gate of the gelding corral and pointed to Ornery George and said, "That's a nice one. Well built. Good eye."

I later found out that he didn't prefer Ornery George at all.

"He's not for a beginner," said Daddy. "Which is not to say—"

"Does your girl here ride him?"

"She has," said Daddy. At this point I fully expected to be told to mount up.

Jem Jarrow said, "Mind if I feel him over?"

"Not all all," said Daddy.

"Mind if I catch him up?"

"You seem like an experienced horseman."

"Done ranch work all my life."

"I guess it's okay, then. If Jake Morrisson recommends—"

"Lemme get my headstall."

He came back from his truck with a rope halter attached to an especially long lead rope. He opened the gate and let himself into the gelding corral. Black George, Socks George, and Ornery George noticed him right away, but after a moment, they went back to eating their hay. He stood there. Pretty soon, one by one, they looked up from their hay. Black George came over to him, and he stroked his head by the eye and ear and down the cheek. Black George let out a snuffle. Now Socks George had to see what was going on, and since he was a little bossy, he came over and pushed Black George out of the way with a quick pinning of the ears. Black George stepped back. Jem gave Socks George a few strokes, too, but when Socks George pushed at him with his nose, he used the head-stall he had in his hand to wave him off.

In the meantime, Ornery George was standing off at a distance. After watching for a minute, he moved around so that his rump faced us and went back to eating. Jem lifted his hand. The other two horses, who had been nosing him, moved off, and then, with Socks George in the lead, they trotted off and swept around in a big arc. It was as if they didn't want to get too far away from Jem. When they came close, he waved them off, but when they got to a certain distance from him, they turned. Pretty soon, he had moved away from the gate toward the middle of the corral and they were going around him in a ragged circle. After they made one circuit, they swept up Ornery George, who just couldn't seem to resist. Now all three trotted around in a leisurely way, not afraid or excited, just, it appeared, willing to move. Every so often, one of them kicked out at another, but not as if he really meant it. They actually seemed to be enjoying themselves.

After they had gone around maybe four times, Jem started stepping backward and to his right. Almost immediately, Black George turned toward him, his ears pricked. The other two were clumsier, but they followed his lead. Then Jem stepped to the left, switched his rope hand, swung his rope, and they were off again, trotting around him, this time going the other direction, Black George in the lead. Two times around, and he stepped back and let them relax. As soon as he did, they came right up to him, and he put his hand on Ornery George. The other two tried to push in, but he lifted his hand and they backed off.

All this time, Daddy was trying hard not to say anything. I

could see all of the thoughts running through his mind—these are my horses, what's he doing, I don't know if I like this, it seems okay, should I stop him, should I ask a question, hmm. Then Jem Jarrow slipped the headstall over Ornery George's head, turned, and walked briskly toward the gate, with Ornery George right on his heels. He stopped once, lifted his hand, and Ornery George stopped, too, and lifted his head. After that, the horse kept his distance a little better. When Jem got to the gate, he said to Daddy, "Would you mind, just for a few minutes, if I used that pen where the colt is? Just to feel this fellow out a bit. I never like to get on a horse until I get to know him a little."

"That makes sense," said Daddy, then, "Abby, put the colt in the first stall."

That's what I did. I was proud of the fact that Jack met me at the gate and walked quietly enough to the stall. I took him all the way in and turned him around, then gave him a few strokes before taking off the halter. As soon as I went out of the stall, he put his head over the door and stared at Jem and Ornery George. It was as if none of the horses could get enough of Jem Jarrow.

Ornery George and Jem were standing in the middle of Jack's pen. George was facing me, and Jem had his back to me. He had his left hand on the lead rope, a few inches below George's chin. The other hand was holding the other end of the lead rope, and maybe a foot and a half of it hung down. What Jem did now was to lift George's chin up and back, toward his (George's) shoulder, while swinging the other end of the rope. George stood there, twisted awkwardly for a moment, and then his hind end moved to the right, away, so that he was more comfortable. Jem released the halter hand, petted George once on the neck, and then did it again. This time I was looking at them from the side. I saw that after the moment of hesitation, what happened was that George's hind foot, the one closest to Jem, stepped under his belly and crossed in front of his other hind foot. Then the other hind foot stepped over, too. It was like a dance step, where you step over your left foot in front of your right and then bring your right foot around.

Jem asked Ornery George to do this three more times. On the third time, as soon as he lifted the hand near the halter, George stepped over behind. Jem said, "There's a fellow," and gave him a good pat down the neck. Then he went around to the other side of the horse, switched hands, and did the same thing but in the opposite direction. George was better at it in this direction and moved over twice, with hardly any pressure, almost immediately.

I had never seen any of this stuff before, and I watched as carefully as I could, because I knew without being told that this was what Mom and Danny had worked out between them.

Now Jem waved the end of the rope, and George went around him in a tight circle, a few times one way, then a few times the other. He was clumsy at it and stiff. Jem had to insist, but eventually, he got it, and he got less awkward.

Jem led the horse to the gate.

I looked at Daddy. He looked like he didn't quite know what to say. Jem said, "Athletic horse, Mr. Lovitt. Nice-made horse. Don't know much about using his body at this point. How old did you say he was?"

"He's six."

"Young, then."

Now he stood George up and ran his hands down his front legs, feeling his knees and fetlocks and hooves. Then he ran his hand down George's spine, pressing here and there. At one point George flinched and tried to step away, right when Jem had his hand where Uncle Luke's rope had been. I thought Jem might ask a question or say something, but he just ran his hand farther down and pressed again. Then he put one hand over George's nose and the other hand on his neck and shifted his head back and forth. He didn't once look at his teeth. All the horses were staring at him. Jack called out from his stall, as if to say, "Look at me! I'm here! I'm the important one, don't you know that?"

Finally, Jem Jarrow walked over to the gate. He said, "Mr. Lovitt, what are you planning to do with this horse, if I might ask?"

"Well, we're getting him ready to be sold, so—"

But really, of course, he didn't have an answer for this question.

Jem said, "I'd like to ride the horse, but I'm wondering if I might come back another day, say, Wednesday? And, if you don't mind, you might just leave the horse alone until then."

I said, "We don't mind."

Daddy said, "Wednesday, Mrs. Lovitt and I will be at the church, setting up—"

I piped up. "I'll be here. I can watch for you, Mr. Jarrow, and help you with whatever you need."

"That's fine. That would be fine," said Jem Jarrow, and even though Daddy didn't look one hundred percent happy about it, he was stuck. And so he smiled and made the best of it.

It was fine with me not to ride Ornery George for another four days.

In the meantime, school was no better than home. In fact, school was so bad that the only thing I enjoyed about it was things we were doing in class—in history we were studying the missions, and I was making a clay model of the mission at San Juan Bautista with one of the boys in my class, Kyle Gonzalez, the sort of kid who is very quiet and always does a good job. In English, we finished with *Adam Bede*, to everyone's relief, and we were reading *The Witch of Blackbird Pond*, which was pretty good. In math, we were making graphs. This is how bad things were with Gloria, Stella, and the Big Four—anything that was a break from them was good. I even tried being friends with Alexis and Barbara and Debbie, but Debbie and I had been bored with each other for four years. Alexis and Barbara were nice enough to me, but they were much more interested in a play they were trying out for at the community theater. It was called *Twelfth Night*, and they were hoping to play a set of twins—Alexis would play the boy and Barbara would play the girl. They couldn't stop talking about this play, which I had never heard of, and they were both afraid of horses, so we didn't have much to say to one another.

As for Stella and the Big Four, you could only call it a war. Brian Connelly was the prize. I couldn't figure out why it should be Brian—there were several boys in our class and in the eighth grade who were cooler and better-looking, but he was the one they were fighting over, and he made it worse by trying to be nice to everyone—he must have talked to some grown-up about it, and that's what they told him to do. Every morning before class, he would stop at each locker—each of the Big Four, Stella, Gloria, and me, for sure, but sometimes also Debbie and Maria and Alexis and Barbara—and say something or other, even if it was only that today, his mom had fixed him tuna fish salad, with celery but not pickles, because he didn't like pickles at all. Our lockers were alphabetical, so his progress ran Mary A., Joan, Stella, Maria, Linda, the twins, Gloria, me, Mary N., Debbie, Fatima, Lucia. Stella and the Big Four kept track of how long he spent with each girl. Of our group, he spent the shortest time with me, and that was good. Usually, he said, "Hey, Abby, how ya doin'?" and I said, "Fine, thanks." It was this, and only this, that prevented the Big Four from focusing on me. If Brian wanted to talk to Stella about *The Munsters*, which was one of his favorite shows, then he might only say a word or two to Mary A. and Joan about what he'd had for breakfast and not even get to Mary N. For the rest of the day, the Big Four would monopolize Brian, and also criticize Stella, by saying things like, "Do those socks match, Stella? In this light, they look different," or, "Did you know you have a little zit, Stella, right there beside your nose? I'm just telling you in case you didn't know." This would be said in a loud voice.

If Brian spent more time with Mary A., looking into her lunch box and admiring what her mother had sent, and didn't get to Stella, then Stella (and sometimes Gloria) played their own games, and one of these was to ask Mary N. if she was losing weight. "You look thinner in the face," was what Stella said, knowing perfectly well that the very thing Mary N. wanted above all things was to look thinner in the face—she had dimples in both cheeks. When they were really mad, they said, "You should wear your skirts shorter." We all knew that Mary N. had fat knees. They said these things in a sweet way, as if they wanted to be friends with Mary N. Since she was the least big of the Big Four, she was the easiest to pick on. Once, when Gloria went to Stella's house for a sleepover, she and Stella called Mary N. twice and asked, "Is your nose running? Better catch it!" They disguised their voices, then laughed and hung up. Gloria told me about this when she called the next night, Saturday. I knew I was supposed to laugh, but I didn't. I didn't like the Big Four, but I wasn't sure who was being meaner. Even so, I didn't think there was anyone to be friends with besides Gloria, and if she liked Stella, then I was stuck with her, too, wasn't I?

On that Monday after Jem Jarrow, everything was quiet for almost the whole day. Even at lunch, they sat at their table and we sat at ours, and the two tables might not have even been in the same universe. Brian had begun his day by chatting with Mary A. and Joan about watching *Mister Ed* the night before. I had never seen *Mister Ed*—even if we'd had TV, the show was on Sunday—but I knew Mister Ed was a talking horse. I had heard Brian say that they got the horse to move his lips by rubbing peanut butter on his gums, and I thought that was interesting. Worth a try, too. But apparently, this conversation was so involving that Brian never did get to Stella, even to say hi, and so she was mad about it for the rest of the day. Then, when Brian came a little late into the lunchroom, Joan and Mary A.

waved at him and moved over to make a spot. Brian hesitated, but he didn't actually look at us. He just sat down.

The problem came in study hall, last period, which normally our class did not have. But our science teacher was sick, so we were sent to study hall with the other seventh graders—no doubt they didn't trust the boys to leave the gas jets alone in the absence of the teacher. Anyway, about five minutes after the bell, our group filed into the study hall and took whatever seats were available, and by the time Mary A. and Joan got into the room (they had been brushing their hair in the girls' bathroom), there was one chair by the window and another by the door, and that one was right next to Stella. I had snagged a chair just behind Stella, and we had already passed our first note—something from her to me, which I hadn't had time to open yet. Joan sat in the chair near us and gave me a look, then gave Stella a look. Then she sighed and opened her science book and began writing a note, which she passed to Debbie, who passed it to Jesús Valdez, who passed it to Fatima, who passed it to Mary N., who passed it to Mary A. So far, so good.

But when Mary A. had completed her response, the teacher just happened to get up and walk around to make sure we were all doing our work, as she sometimes did, and so there was a new challenge. Mary A. and Joan met this challenge by deciding to sharpen their pencils, which they were allowed to do without asking permission, and so they both got up, pretending not to be paying any attention to one another, and headed for the pencil sharpener next to the blackboard. As soon as Joan got up, I saw that Stella was fiddling with something, and then, before Joan even got to the pencil sharpener,

I saw what it was—she had removed the cartridge from her fountain pen (black ink, because we were required to turn in final copies of our papers in black ink) and leaned over and set it on Joan's desk chair.

Now Joan sharpened her pencil, exchanged her note with Mary A., and headed back to her seat. I was looking at the cartridge. I was sure she would see it—it was sitting right there as big as anything. But she was too busy making faces across the room at Mary A. and Linda, and so she turned around, twisted her body, and sat right on it. And then she slid around to get more comfortable. I looked at Stella, who was smiling and reading her history book. Stella didn't look at me. Everyone else was studying hard. Even Debbie had her nose so deep in her book that I couldn't see it. I didn't know whether Stella knew that I had seen the cartridge.

Joan wasn't wearing a white skirt, but it wasn't black, either—she had a new mossy green wool skirt with pleats that were sewn to about four inches below the waist, and then flared out. It was pretty, and her sweater matched it. She also had on a white blouse. When the bell rang and she stood up, she had a long streak of black ink running across her skirt and then down. When she reached around to smooth her skirt after standing up, she got the ink on her fingers and then on her sweater. It was then she noticed the ink. She screamed and started cursing. She said the G word attached to the D word, and more than once. Very bad. Stella made no sound or gesture. She didn't even ask what happened. She just wandered out of the room with the boys. The boys didn't care, but all the girls except Debbie, who was already out the door, gathered around Joan and looked at her skirt, her hand, and her sweater. "Oh, it's ruined!" cried Joan.

Linda found the ink cartridge under the desk chair. The desk chair had a streak on it, too. Joan insisted that someone had left it there on purpose, but the other girls didn't believe this—any one of the boys, they thought, could have forgotten that he dropped the ink cartridge or dropped it without realizing it. It could have been there for hours or all day.

I was the only one who knew that Stella had put it there on purpose.

After school I was waiting for the bus with Gloria, who had been sitting in her usual seat in the front of the study hall, under the gaze of the teacher, and so didn't know anything about the skirt incident. She and I were watching the other girls. Stella had, once again, gotten picked up by her mom. Gloria said, "I don't see why it's such a big deal. She got ink on her skirt, so what? Her mom will take it to the cleaners."

I said, "I guess it was a new skirt."

"Stella said that. She said they were talking about it at lunch, that it was a new skirt from some store in San Francisco."

"She heard that?"

"She said she did."

I said, "You know, I—" but I said it quietly, because I wasn't sure how to tell Gloria about Stella. Gloria didn't even hear me. She exclaimed, "Forget them! Can I come see the colt this weekend? I saved him some apples."

"He doesn't eat treats yet."

"Well, I'll give them to the others, then. But we can do something after. I'll get Mom to bring me out for a while, then you can get your mom to let us go someplace for the afternoon."

"I'll ask."

So, I didn't say a word about what I'd seen, but all the way home on the bus, I thought about how mean Stella had been. I wondered if the ink on the skirt equaled the pen tear in the stocking. I also wondered when Joan was going to realize that Stella had done it on purpose and whether Stella wanted Joan to know that. After all, what good was it, in terms of the war, if Joan thought it was an accident?

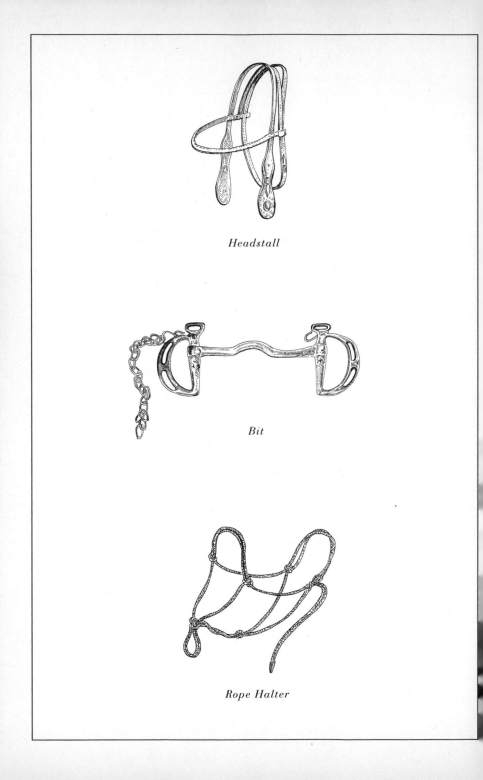

Headstall

Bit

Rope Halter

Chapter 12

On Wednesday after school, I changed into my riding clothes right away and was on Black George when Daddy and Mom left for the church. As soon as they turned right out of the driveway, I jumped off him and put him back in the gelding corral—he was a willing horse, and Daddy always said, "Some days, ten good minutes is enough."

I still didn't quite know what was going on about Jem Jarrow, but I had some suspicions—Danny worked for Jake Morrisson, Jake Morrisson knew Jem Jarrow, Jake Morrisson and Mom had had a long talk, Mom had hurried Daddy out to the church, telling him something that I didn't understand about the chairs, and maybe the windows needed cleaning, too, since no one had touched them since the fall, and cleanliness was next to godliness, and when Daddy said, "Why today?" Mom said, "Next week is Mrs. Larkin and Mrs. Lodge doing the chairs, and after that the Greeleys, so if we don't do it, it won't get done." They packed up the Windex and some rags and off they went.

Jem Jarrow's truck turned in the driveway moments later. I ran to meet it.

Jem Jarrow wasn't much of a smiler, but he had a cheerful face. When he got out, I saw again that he was small—maybe half a head taller than I was at the most—I had forgotten that and been thinking of him as Daddy's size. And you could see the horizon between his knees, as Daddy would say. Being bowlegged was, according to Daddy, the first sign of a horseman, because to get that way, you had to fit your legs around the horse from an early age. Jem said, "How do, Abby. Been well?"

And I said, "Yes, sir, how about you?"

"Can't complain," said Jem Jarrow.

That was it for the formalities. I followed him out to the gelding corral. The horses all looked up at once and stared right at him. Just as before, but for not quite as long a time, he stopped and watched them.

I said, "What are you looking for?"

"How they are. How they feel about each other."

"What do you make of that?"

"Well, first off, I'm just curious. Always been curious. When I was in school, they told me not to ask so many questions, so I learned to keep my mouth shut and my eyes peeled. But more than that, right now, I wonder how this

144

gelding we're working with gets along with the others. I see both this time and the last time that he's quick to take offense. That other one, the dark one, he's more easygoing, but he's more athletic, too. So, all in all, I suspect that the dark one—"

"That's Black George."

"—is the boss of the three of them, but he spends less time thinking about it than our friend."

"Some kids are just cool."

"That's right."

I laughed.

By now, we were standing at the gate, and Jem opened it and walked in. The first thing he did was wave the horses away and walk to the center of the corral, where he got them going around him again. They all did it more smoothly than the last time, to the right and then to the left and then back to the right. By the time he let them turn in toward him, they were one hundred percent relaxed, as far as I could tell.

Ornery George didn't act as though he knew this session was about him. He was just curious and sniffing, like the others, until Jem put his hand on his neck, and then the horse's ears flicked backward and his eyes sort of narrowed. But Jem acted as if he didn't notice this and put his hand on the bridge of George's nose, about halfway between the nostrils and the eyes. They stood there. Jem didn't pet George as I would have done. He just stood there with his right hand on George's neck and his left hand over the bridge of George's nose. After some time, George's neck loosened and his head dropped. Just then,

Jem gave him a pat on the neck. While George's head was still lowered, Jem pulled up the headstall and fastened it together. Then he turned and walked briskly back to the gate. George followed him. George had a look on his face that wasn't willingness, I would say, but also not grumpiness. More than anything, it was curiosity. I shooed the other horses back and held open the gate. Man and horse walked through and headed to the arena.

Jem and George went about a third of the way into the arena, to the most open spot, and at a wave of Jem's hand, George started trotting around him in a tight circle, tighter than in the corral, just right around Jem. Since the other horses weren't with him, though, he must have decided that it wasn't much fun, because he kept trying to stop. Jem wouldn't let him. Every time he tried to stop, Jem waved him forward again with his free hand while lifting the hand that was holding the rope. Jem wasn't going to let George stop until he did something, and what that thing was, I saw a moment later, was that dance step—cross his inside hind leg over the outside hind leg and bring his hindquarters around to the outside. When he did that, Jem let him stop, then he waved him in the other direction, in the same tight circle. Once again, he was reluctant to move and awkward until he crossed those hind legs, inside to outside. At the same time as the legs crossed, George's head and neck dropped and relaxed, and his progress around the circle was easier.

I climbed up on the fence. I was glad I had my hat on, because it was a sunny afternoon, nice and warm across the top of my back. I could see from there that the geldings and the mares had decided that whatever was going on didn't concern them, and so they had gone back to eating their hay, but Jack, in his pen, was all eyes. He stood with his chest against the fence and his ears pricked. A couple of times when George changed direction, Jack snorted and humped his back. It was cute.

After a couple of minutes, Jem let George stop trotting around him. Now he stepped up right beside him again, where he was standing, and he used that lifting motion on the rope. George had to step his hind end over as soon as he felt the upward pressure, but I have to say that he didn't learn this smoothly, or without protest. Especially when he was stepping to the left, he tried more than once to pull his head away or simply to stiffen and wait until Jem Jarrow would give up.

But Jem Jarrow was a patient man. That was the complete difference between him and Uncle Luke. You had the feeling that Jem would stand there all day with the rope lifted, waiting for the horse to put two and two or, for that matter, one and one together. If he did, he got a pat. If he didn't, he didn't get anything—they just waited. Uncle Luke, I knew, and maybe even Daddy, would have said something, or batted the animal, or given him a push. I could see that Jem Jarrow wanted George to think of this thing himself, to not be told every time what to do.

They must have worked on this for five or ten minutes. Another thing they did was Jem just put his hand over the bridge of George's nose and pulled it around so his neck was curved to the left and down. A couple of times, Jem released his hold, and George's head popped back to the front, as if on a spring. But then he did the right thing—he just relaxed and kept his head turned even after Jem had taken away his hand. It was then that George got the pat.

I shouted, "What's that for?"

Jem said, "The horse doesn't know how to soften."

"Is that because people were mean to him?"

"Don't know."

"But—"

Jem stopped working the horse for a moment and waved me over to him. I jumped off the fence. The sand in the arena was moist and springy. Perfect, really. When I got to the two of them, Jem didn't do what I thought he would do, which was to ask me if people had been mean to the horse, he said, "Here's how I think of it, Abby. When the horse knows how to soften and go along and be happy doing it, then it won't matter to him what happened before, and if it doesn't matter to him, then it doesn't matter to me, either."

He handed me the rope.

I was to stand just to the side of George's neck with my hand up by the halter and the rope coming up through it like a rein. At the same time that I lifted the rope, twisting the horse's head and neck upward a bit, I was to put my other hand on George's shoulder about halfway up to the withers and push steadily, but not hard. As soon as I felt George's shoulder loosen and release, I was to stop everything and give him a little pat. To be frank, I didn't see the point of this, but I did it three times and then a fourth. Each time, I felt George's body start out stiff and then soften up. Jem said, "See all these muscles, from the chest to the tail? All along the shoulder and the ribs and the flanks? And then this other set, all down his back and over his croup?" His hand feathered along George's spine for a moment. "If all those muscles are loose, he'll be easy to ride and he'll enjoy himself. If they're all tight, he'll be hard to ride and dangerous, too, because even if he doesn't go against you, his balance won't be good, and his mind won't be on what you want him to do. He'll be looking for a reason to rebel, or to spook, or to stumble."

"How can he look for a reason to stumble?"

"If his body is stiff, he won't pick up his feet very well, and so a little something on the ground that he would be aware of if he were supple will cause him to stumble."

He showed me how to get George to come around me, and then I set myself up so I could feel the other side tense and soften. He said, "When he steps his back feet under and across, he has to use all those muscles I was telling you about, especially the back muscles. It's easier to use them if they're supple, not stiff, so he learns to soften them when you ask, because he really wants to do things the easy way. And it's actually easier for him to get along with you and do what you say and not buck you off, but you have to show him how to do it before he knows that."

He took the rope back from me and went right in front of George, maybe three feet out. He said, "Here's another little test." He raised both his hands, both his index fingers, and waved them at George, as if to say, Naughty, naughty. But what he wanted George to do was step back. George wasn't sure that he himself wanted to step back, so he leaned back and then leaned farther back, without moving his feet. His ears were out to either side and a little back, what Daddy and I called "I can't hear you" ears. When Jem put his hands down, George stood up straight again. This time, Jem raised his left hand and then, with his right hand down low, used the lead rope to suddenly pop George under the chin. George threw up his head and stepped back. Jem patted him on the forehead. Then they did it again. It took three times, but on the fourth time, Jem lifted his fingers, and George stepped back one step without being popped under the chin. Jem said, "Horses don't like to back up, generally. There's no eyes back there."

I laughed.

"But when he backs up, once again, he's got to be soft all over to do it. So it's a good test. I don't get on without giving him that little test. If he won't back up, then we work a little more."

"Don't you ever get on a horse without giving him tests?"

"Not unless we're good friends of long standing."

The next thing Jem did was hand me George's rope and go get the tack. I just stood there, because I didn't want to do the wrong thing, and I noticed that George just stood there, too, which was an accomplishment for Ornery George. I gave him a little pat on the nose. I couldn't help myself.

Jem was small, but he carried his saddle like every cowboy I'd ever seen, over his hip, with the cinch folded over the seat of the saddle and the stirrups hanging. A western saddle is heavy. Daddy always carried his on one side one day and on the other side the next day so as to exercise his back evenly. When Jem swung the saddle up on George, George stepped away. Jem took it off, swung it up again. George stepped away. Jem took it off, swung it up again. George must have seen that resistance was futile, and so the last time, he stood there. Jem went around and arranged the cinch, then he came around again and gestured for me to hand him the lead rope. When I gave it to him, he laid it over his forearm. I saw that he wasn't going to make George do anything at all, but instead, he was going to have him stand there of his own accord while Jem was going about his business. After the saddle was cinched up, Jem asked George to make some tight circles again, this time with the cinch tight and the stirrups flapping. At first, it was hard for George—he was stiff and kind of mad, but then he got used to it. I ran to get the bridle.

When I passed Jack, he whinnied at me, and I stopped to give him a pat on the neck. His neck was almost shed out, and his coat was dark and shiny.

Jem went about getting George to take the bit in the same way he had done with the halter—he put his hand over the bridge of George's nose. George was to bend his neck and drop his head and relax so that Jem could slip the bit into his mouth and pull the crown piece over his ears. It took a minute or two to get this done, but not as long as before. I said, "Is he smart?"

"All horses are smart. How else would they be able to work for a living? They've got jobs to do, and most do them."

"Daddy says they only understand the carrot or the stick."

Jem laughed. He said, "Generally, I don't use either a carrot or a stick. Seems like most horses remember the stick better than they remember the carrot."

"What do you use, then?"

"I use curiosity."

I could see that.

"A horse is a curious fellow. Even when he knows he shouldn't go look at something, chances are his curiosity will get the best of him, and he will at least walk toward it. Hardest horse to train is a horse who isn't interested in anything new or is always afraid, but this horse isn't like that. He's of two minds."

"Mom says curiosity killed the cat."

"When does she say that?"

"When someone is asking too many questions."

"Someone like you?"

"No. Someone like Danny."

Jem laughed again and said, "I can see that."

Then he said, "But horses aren't cats. Horses in the wild have to keep an eye out and be ready to investigate and know what should be in their world and what shouldn't be. They have to make up their minds. So they're always looking, and that's a sign of intelligence. Lots of people don't give them much credit for intelligence, but I don't agree with that. If your horse is curious about you, then the first step is made. When he satisfies his curiosity and finds something interesting and fun going on, then likely he'll want to join the fun."

After softening George in the saddle and bridle in the way that he had previously done in just the halter, Jem squared him up and mounted. He mounted with no apparent effort—it was like he had springs in his heels. Just watching that, I knew that getting on and off a horse was as automatic for Jem Jarrow as walking. Then he didn't ride off immediately. It was only after sitting there for a moment that he asked George to walk on.

Stepping over, stepping over, stepping over, that little dance step—for a while, that was all they did. Finally, they trotted around in a circle. George had his head low and to the inside, and his inside back hoof went in the print of his outside front hoof. They went around a couple of times like that and then turned, step step step, the hind legs crossing, and went back the other way. Then they cantered. George was good for about halfway around the arena, and then he remembered who he was and started to put his head down. Just then, Jem used his inside rein to lift George's head up and to the inside. George softened, turned, and cantered on, no longer thinking of bucking. This happened twice. Otherwise, they wove around the jumps and barrels in the arena, at the trot and then the canter and then back to the trot, always changing what they were doing, what direction they were going. Ornery George, I could see, had given up.

When they were walking around, catching their breath, I said, "But a little girl can't ride him."

Jem Jarrow smiled. He said, "Maybe not today. But soon."

I believed him. But I was glad that "soon" wasn't "now."

We cooled George out, and brushed him down, and put

him with the other geldings. Jem shook my hand and thanked me, got in his truck, and drove off. I didn't know what the next step was, but I was sure Mom had a plan. I watered and hayed all the horses and gave Jack his rubdown. It was getting dark when Daddy and Mom drove in.

We had to eat supper in a hurry because we had to get back to the church. Mom made pigs in a blanket and coleslaw. While we were eating, Daddy ran down the list: did I check the horses' water?

Yes.

Did I give everyone their hay?

Yes.

Were the stalls clean from the weekend?

Yes.

Was all the tack put away?

Yes.

Were all the gates closed and locked?

Yes.

Did this fellow Jem Jarrow look like he was going to buy the horse?

I glanced at Mom, who lifted one eyebrow but didn't say anything.

I said, "He went nicely for him. He wasn't ornery at all."

"Hmm," said Daddy, smiling. But then he said, "He doesn't look like he can pay much. Mr. Tacker—"

But Mr. Tacker hadn't called. I said, "We didn't talk about that."

"I didn't expect you would."

There was a silence, and then Daddy said, "Well, you can't

count on a thing. For every buyer, there are ten lookers. I wish I'd been here for the tryout, though."

"It went fine," I said.

For the rest of the week, Daddy didn't say another thing about Jem Jarrow. I suppose he figured that Jem was just another buyer who'd gone elsewhere.

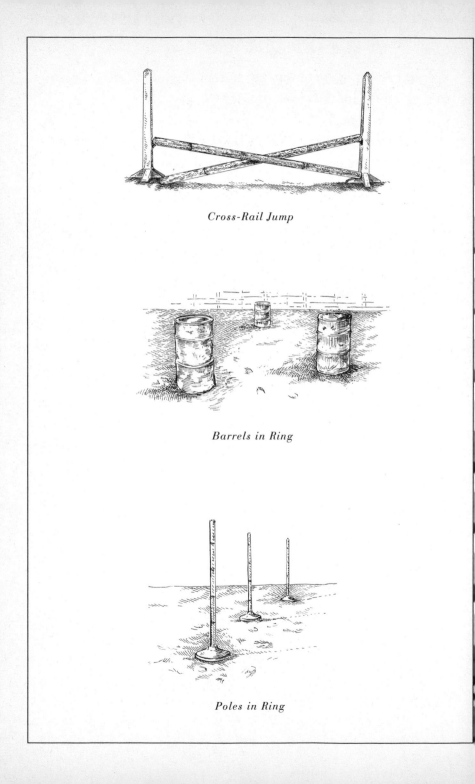

Cross-Rail Jump

Barrels in Ring

Poles in Ring

Chapter 13

ALL THAT WEEK, THERE WAS A LULL IN THE WAR AT SCHOOL. FOR one thing, lots of kids were out with a virus, including Brian Connelly and Mary A.

Kyle Gonzalez and I worked steadily on our model. There was going to be a big display of all the mission models in the cafeteria lasting for the rest of the school year. Ours was the only one made of clay. We finished the church and the walls around the courtyard and the bell tower. The art teacher gave me a piece of green cloth for the grass in the courtyard, and I cut trees out of cardboard and colored them on both sides. Kyle found some little Christmas bells somewhere and set them into the arches of the bell tower with bent pins. If you hit one of them with your pencil, it would ring. When we were finished on Friday afternoon, everything was painted a light color—not white, because Kyle didn't think that white was the right color, but sort of a pinky-gray-cream that was the best we could do.

The missions would be set up in the lunchroom in order, south to north, on a long map of California cut out of brown paper and laid across three tables. The first one was San Diego de Alcala, and the last one was San Francisco Solano. San Juan Bautista was number 15. I didn't know a thing about saints or missions, but I thought all the models were pretty. I had thought all those places—San Jose, San Luis Obispo, San Francisco—were just cities, but they were people, too. In our family, we never talked about saints or missions or Catholics, really, so I hadn't thought much about it.

There was going to be a parents' night during which everyone was supposed to come to look at our models of the missions, but that would be on Wednesday, so we wouldn't be able to come, and so I didn't tell Daddy and Mom about it at all. I wondered if, four years ago, Danny hadn't done the exact same thing.

In the meantime, at home, I rode all the horses other than Ornery George and I did my jobs and everything was quiet. On Friday night, the phone rang, and it was Miss Slater, inviting me to come to their barn. Melinda, she said, wanted to see me, and Miss Slater thought we might have fun—Gallant Man was in great shape. I would have a jumping lesson on him (there was a show in two and a half weeks) and then Melinda would have a little jumping lesson on him, too. She could watch me and then try it herself.

Gloria was never opposed to going out there. When I called her, she said her mother would drive us. That way, we could stop for supper at her house, and they would bring me back about nine. Mom and Daddy agreed to all of this, as long as I rode Black George, Blue Jewel, Socks George, and Star Jewel first thing in the morning.

Gloria and her mother showed up about eleven. They had on cowboy boots and cowboy hats, and bandannas around their necks. They wore matching shirts with bucking horses and lariats all over them. They waited while I changed into my English riding clothes, and we got into the car.

It was a beautiful day. Even the pine forest around the stable was bright with sunshine. Gallant Man was all tacked up, and he looked really cute, so cute that after I was on him, Gloria's mom took pictures of us (then she took pictures of everyone else, including Miss Slater, who sat sideways on the fence with a whip in her hand and her tall boots crossed at the ankles) and Melinda, who was perfectly turned out, as always.

My part of the jumping lesson went fine. Miss Slater was in a good mood, and Gallant Man was very gallant. He trotted or cantered down to every jump with his ears pricked, and he came up under me each time in exactly the same way. The only bad thing he did was after the second and third jump, when he bucked a little bit and tossed his head. I knew it was from high spirits, so I just turned him and went on. He didn't do it again.

Once was enough. When I brought him over to Melinda at the side of the arena, she shook her head. Miss Slater kept smiling and said, "Come on, now, Melinda. You rode him yesterday, and you said you liked it."

"He wasn't bucking yesterday."

"He's not really bucking today, is he, Abby?"

"He was happy," I said. "That's all."

"I don't want him to be happy." Then she changed her mind. "I mean, I don't want him to be extra happy."

Gloria said, "You're a good rider, Melinda. I saw you. You're way better than I am, and I would ride him. You don't have to worry."

Melinda didn't say anything.

I gave Gallant Man some pats. He snorted away a fly, which startled Melinda, but he was otherwise being good. What I really wanted to do was ask Melinda what had happened that had made her so scared, but I remembered Jem Jarrow saying that things that have happened don't really matter to a horse, so I thought, well, maybe the same thing worked for people. I took Melinda's hand and said, "Let's walk around with the pony awhile." Miss Slater caught my eye and smiled. I said to Melinda, "You go on the left side and I'll go on the right, and the pony will walk between us."

We did this, both of us holding a rein, with Melinda also holding the end of the reins so that they wouldn't drag on the ground. When we were at the far end of the ring, as far as we could get from Miss Slater, Melinda suddenly said, "It's only when I get here that I get afraid. When I'm at home, I always think it's going to be great. You can't believe how many pictures I've drawn all over my notebooks of Gallant Man and how much I think about him, but the closer I come to him, it's like I want to scream."

"That's funny. Not funny ha ha."

"I know."

"Do you come out here every day?"

"Every day they let me. That's almost every day. My mom says I'm too grumpy if I don't come out."

I said, "You're weird, Melinda," not as if I meant it, but as if I were just joking with her, and Melinda gave me a big grin.

She said, "I know that." We walked on. At the end of the arena, we turned and headed back toward Miss Slater and Gloria. Melinda said, "If I get on now, will you walk along with us? You don't have to lead me."

I gave her a leg up. Once she had settled into the saddle and I had shortened the stirrups, she sat up and put her heels down. Her position was very good. We walked along. The pony behaved himself. Finally, I said, "Has the pony ever done anything bad?"

"No."

"Then why do you think he will?"

"I don't know."

"I don't think he will. He never did anything bad with me, either. Some horses just don't do anything bad. It's like a habit that they don't have."

"Like not sucking your thumb."

"Yeah. Exactly. Kids who don't suck their thumbs just don't suck their thumbs." I stepped a little away from the pony and let her handle the reins. She turned him, and I followed. I thought that was a good sign. Then she turned him again. She was riding him, but it was like she didn't even realize it. She said, "I've got pictures of him on the lid of my desk, so when I open it, there he is. And I wrote two stories about him for school." She was smiling. A moment later, she trotted away, but then she stopped because I didn't trot after her.

I trotted after her. Then I got an idea.

She was looking at me. When I trotted past her, she nudged the pony up into the trot again, and they followed me, about ten feet behind. I jogged down the long side of the arena, then rounded the corner. They were right behind me. I jogged diagonally across the arena. They were right behind me. I turned right. They turned right. I turned right again and trotted over a tiny cross-rail, not more than six inches off the ground. They were right behind me. I didn't even look back, I just swung around and trotted over it again, then I turned right and trotted over another one. By this time, I was out of breath, so I stopped. Melinda and the pony came up to me. I thought of Jem Jarrow and how he gave George one pat but didn't make a big deal. I said, "That was good!" but nothing more. It occurred to me that when you make a big deal rather than a little deal of someone doing something, maybe they think you're also telling them that you never thought they could do it.

I walked over to Gloria and Miss Slater and Gloria's mom, where they were standing together watching us. Miss Slater was grinning, but as we approached, she calmed down, gave me a nod, and walked toward the center of the arena. Melinda and the pony followed her, and then they started having a regular lesson. Melinda did fine and seemed happy. It was like she had been under a spell, and now the spell was broken. Anyway, the lesson even included trotting back and forth over the two sets of cross-rails. We just watched. Melinda's mom smiled but didn't say anything. She must have thought it was very cold, because she had a black wool coat on, gloves, and a fur hat.

Miss Slater was beaming. After the groom came out and led Melinda and the pony away to be untacked, she held out her hand to me and said, "Abby, my dear, you are a natural. I want to thank you."

I held out my hand. She shook it and put her other hand on my shoulder.

It wasn't until we were in the car that Gloria and her mom

162

started talking about Melinda. I gathered that while I was riding the pony, they had learned a lot about Mr. and Mrs. Anniston. Melinda was an only child. Mr. Anniston was twenty years older than Mrs. Anniston, and he had children from his first marriage who were almost the same age as Mrs. Anniston.

Anyway, the really important thing that they had learned from Miss Slater, who obviously was "talking out of school" as Mom would say because she didn't like gossip, was that the Annistons were "estranged."

I couldn't imagine what this meant. Certainly Melinda was strange, or "weird," but she seemed proud to be weird. As I listened, I learned that one symptom of being estranged was that one parent lived in the "vacation home" and one parent lived in the "primary residence," but according to Miss Slater, with the Annistons, you couldn't tell the difference between the two—one was in Los Angeles and the other one was here, and both were very splendid.

"One of them has to be sold, though," said Gloria's mother, "to pay for the divorce. Martha Slater says that Melinda doesn't know a thing about it yet."

"I won't tell."

"I didn't think you would, dear, but a word to the wise is always the best policy."

After that, we didn't talk about it.

But neither did we talk about school. I thought we would. In fact, I thought that Gloria had set up this whole invitation so that we could figure out what to do about how awful everything was. Instead, she worked on her model of her mission (San Juan Capistrano), which she was making with Debbie and a couple of the boys. The only thing she had left to do was make little origami birds to represent the swallows. I made a couple for her, but they weren't very good, so she said she would glue them in the back. "Debbie isn't very good at that, either," she said. "But she wrote out the history in fancy writing with red capital letters. That looks nice." We played records on her new hi-fi set. When you folded the turntable up into the box and unplugged the cords, it looked sort of like a suitcase with a handle, so you could take it with you places if you wanted to. Her grandfather had sent it to her for no reason at all, just because he saw it in a store, and he had also sent her two albums, *Beatles '65*, by The Beatles, and another record by a group called The Searchers. I was kind of amazed that a grandfather would do something like that. When my grandparents gave us things, they were old—pictures of what Oklahoma looked like in the early days or a silver belt buckle that had been passed down in the family.

We had fried chicken for dinner, which was very good, a special recipe including cornflakes. It came to me maybe three times to tell Gloria about Stella and the ink cartridge, but in the end I never did. It felt too much like tattling, and anyway, it was possible that Gloria knew all about it and wasn't telling me.

Nor did I tell Mom when she came into my room at bedtime that night. When I told her about Melinda, she said that maybe Melinda was afraid because her family was keeping things from her, so she suspected that there was a lot going on that she didn't know anything about. She said, "Children always know more than you think."

I didn't know if this was true, because I didn't know what Mom and Daddy thought I knew.

I told her about the fried chicken and the origami birds and the new record player.

Just when I thought she was going to leave, she said, "Jem Jarrow had stopped by while you were gone."

"He did?"

"Yes, and your daddy was all set to sell him a horse, but he said that he was never in the market for a horse, and he thought maybe he should clear things up."

"What did he have to clear up?"

"Well, Abby, Danny and Jake sent him over, and I knew about that. It was me who told Jake that you were afraid to ride the horse."

"I told Danny that, too."

"I know. The thing is, Danny has been working with Jem. Jake has known Jem Jarrow for forty years, working around at one ranch or another, and Jake always thought he was the best hand with a horse in the area, but Jem wasn't hiring himself out before. He and his brother had a big ranch, but now they've sold some of the land and some of the cattle, so he thought he would go out and see if there was a living to be made training horses."

"What did Daddy say?"

"He said, 'Not much of one.'"

I sighed. I said, "Daddy never did ask me what happened."

"I think he thought you just stood there while Jem tried the horse. He didn't know that Jem actually did anything with the horse."

"Does he want to know now?"

"Yes."

"Can I tell him tomorrow?" I was really tired.

"Tomorrow is Sunday. What I came up here to tell you, Abby, is that if you would like Jem Jarrow to come back, I

165

think you'd better make your case tonight, before your father has his own thoughts about it and they get set, if you know what I mean."

I knew what she meant. I threw back the covers and put on my robe and slippers. She went out of my room, and I followed her downstairs.

Daddy was sitting at his desk, reading the Bible, when I came in. He always had to do that on Saturday night in order to have a lesson to talk about on Sunday, because our church didn't have a pastor or a minister—the men in the church took turns "talking" about things, which meant that each Sunday, each of them would do a short lesson. The short lessons were supposed to add up to something about as long as a regular church service.

Daddy closed his Bible and pushed it away from himself. Then he turned his chair toward me. I hoped that the lesson he was working on was about forgiveness and mercy rather than justice and wrath, but there was no telling ahead of time. He said, "So, Abby. I guess Jem Jarrow never came to actually buy the horse. I guess your mom and Jake played a trick on me."

I said, "I guess."

"I can't say I like that, but I recognize that 'God resisteth the proud, but giveth grace unto the humble.'"

I guessed that that was going to be his text for the following day. I wasn't quite sure whether he was referring to himself or Ornery George, so I said, "Well, George acted pretty humble after Jem—I mean, Mr. Jarrow—worked with him."

Mom said, "I think it's okay to call him Jem."

Daddy said, "How did he work with him?"

I decided that it was still not the best thing, especially if we

166

were talking about pride, to mention Danny, so I mixed the two up together a bit. "Well, first he got George to do things that he wanted him to do without making a big deal of it. If the horse was coming toward him, he waved him away and made him keep going until *he* said George could stop. Whatever George did, he never let him think it was his own idea. If he wanted to go, Jem made him go faster. If he wanted to stop, Jem didn't let him stop until he had gone farther than he wanted to."

"Hmm," said Daddy.

"Another thing was, he didn't focus on him at first. He worked all the horses together so that George couldn't prepare himself to be ornery. By the time he singled him out, George was ready to do something."

"Why?"

"Well, according to what he said to me, because he had aroused his curiosity. He said horses are very curious."

Daddy opened his mouth to speak.

"And you can use that to get them to do what you want to do. I guess like making something a game."

Mom said, "That always worked with you kids. If you were fussing or crying and I went over and started doing something in your toy box, pretty soon you would stop fussing because you wanted to see what I was doing."

"Like that," I said.

"Hmm," said Daddy.

"But once he got on George, he did make him work. It's just that the work started out with a lot of turns. He said that the horse had to learn to soften and step his hind foot over the instant you asked for it, and if he did, he would be less likely to get stubborn or to stumble." I thought again. "When he was loping and George started to buck, he pulled him up with one rein and over to the inside, not very hard, and George went around a little bit and then loped off. He only tried to buck that one time."

"Well, he's a good rider. He's been riding and working cows all his life, they say."

"I know. But it didn't look that hard."

This was a statement I soon came to repent of.

"I wish he would buy the horse and we could dispense with the whole problem." He sighed.

I said, "I don't want to dispense with the whole problem."

"You don't?"

"I want to try it a couple more times. I want to see if it only works for him."

"Well, I—"

"It was interesting. I watched the whole time." To myself, I added, and I watched Danny, too, and that was interesting, too. I said, "He came twice, right?"

"Yes."

"Well, it seemed to me that the horse learned something from the first time to the second. I always thought that the horse is supposed to do what he's told, but this was different— he did more than what he was told. It was like he remembered what he was told before and didn't have to be told again, only reminded. I bet if Jem came another couple of times, the horse would do what he was told without being told."

Mom said, "You mean he would learn something."

"Yes, that's what I mean."

Daddy said, "I don't really think of horses as having a body of knowledge, but maybe they do."

"They do," I said. "I mean, when George does want to get caught, he's acting like he knows something bad is going to happen, and so he isn't going to cooperate."

"Well, even so, I'm sure Jem Jarrow doesn't train horses for free."

I knew what that meant. It meant that was that. Because if you put a lot of money into a horse, then you couldn't make much of a profit, and if you didn't make much of a profit, then you couldn't buy more horses. Or anything else.

Thinking of Ornery George made me think of something else, though. I said, "Mr. Tacker really liked George. He looked at him three times while he was loading Red Jewel into his trailer. You always said someone will pay more for a pretty one, and he's the prettiest, except for Black George."

"I doubt if Mr. Tacker would think Black George is prettier. Ornery George is about as pretty as they come for a ranch horse. Or a parade horse."

Now was when I buttoned my lip. Because I could see the wheels turning, even though as a little girl, I wasn't supposed to see the wheels turning. Mom said, "Okay, Abby. You go to bed now. I know you're tired."

But I stayed awake for another hour or more, waiting to hear Daddy and Mom go into their room. By the time I fell asleep, they were still up. If they were still up, they would still be talking. If they were still talking, then Daddy hadn't yet said, "I've made up my mind," or, "Who's the boss around here?" If he hadn't said that, then Mom was going to have her way.

Riding Helmet

Farrier Apron Chaps

Tall Boots

Chapter 14

TRAINING SESSIONS WITH JEM JARROW WERE TWELVE DOLLARS apiece, for forty-five minutes. He agreed to come on Monday and Tuesday and then on Saturday. This gave me something to look forward to during school.

After lunch on Monday, the tables in the cafeteria were moved into their new arrangement, six of them in a long line over against the back wall, away from the windows. The teachers then laid out the long sheet of brown paper with the outline of California on it. At each of the spots where the twenty-one missions were to sit, someone had drawn stars, and because some of these were rather close together, someone had drawn arrows to different places on the paper where we were to place our missions. Barbara and Alexis Goldman had made the San Diego

Mission entirely of corks that were cut into chunks and glued together. Two of the missions were made of Lincoln Logs. One was just a pile of stones, and the label read, *The Mission La Purisma was destroyed by an EARTHQUAKE in 1812.* There were some plastic cows and pigs set around the rubble. I doubted that the boys who made that model were going to get As.

Joan, Linda, and the two Marys had gotten permission to collaborate on one mission, Mission San Carlos, in Carmel, because it was big, beautiful, and important. The model sat in the middle of the whole display, about half again as large as any of the others. There was the church, the bell tower, with steps going up around it, and a courtyard. Everything was inside a box, and on the outside of the box, the girls had pasted color photos of things like the garden and the interior of the church, with information about Father Serra and Monterey typed on cards. The buildings were glued together from plywood, with designs painted on them. It took two girls to carry the mission from the social studies room to the lunchroom, and we all had to make way.

Unfortunately, Stella and one of the boys, Larry Schnuck, had constructed Mission San Antonio out of cardboard. It was the next one down from Carmel and looked very poor and small by comparison. And then Miss Albers, who was homeroom teacher for the other seventh grade, said, "Stella, we'll just move yours a little bit to the side so that we can fit Carmel in here." I didn't even have to look at Stella to know what she thought of that.

I made Gloria meet me in the girls' bathroom during study hall. After we pushed on all the stall doors to make sure that no one else was in there, I took her over by the sinks, where we could see someone come in, and I said, "Were you looking at Stella when Miss Albers made her move her mission?"

"No. Some of my birds fell off—"

"Well, she was plenty mad. Her face turned beet red." As I said this, I felt sick to my stomach.

Gloria said, "So what?"

"So what if she does something to that mission?"

"Oh, pullease. You're crazy."

"No, I'm not, but I can't tell you—"

"Well, if you can't tell me, then so what, again. Why can't you tell me?" Her eyebrows lowered and she stared at me. Right then, I knew she knew all about the ink cartridge.

"I saw something that nobody else saw."

Now she looked at me. "What?" But it didn't seem as though she was asking a question. More like she was making a dare—daring me to tell.

I made up my mind right there that Gloria wasn't on my side anymore. "I can't tell." And then I made up my mind that she was.

"Abby, if you brought me in here, you have to tell."

"I haven't told anyone."

"You're kidding. It's that bad?"

It seemed like two halves of me were certain of what I should do. Unfortunately, each half was certain of a different thing. One half was certain that if I told Gloria, she would be shocked at what Stella had done and help me prevent Stella from hurting the Carmel mission. The other half was certain that Gloria and Stella were in on things together, and in that case, I had no idea what I should do. I didn't know if Gloria was more in favor of Stella doing something bad or more against it.

I didn't say anything, and finally, Gloria said, "Oh, for heaven's sake. Who cares?" She sounded fed up. She washed her hands and dried them with some paper towels, then walked out. After that, I sat on the edge of the sink rubbing my stomach in circles, trying to make the feeling go away. I actually said, out loud to myself, "Don't make such a big deal of it! It's not a big deal!" But my stomach thought it was a big deal, and so I was late to algebra. I didn't see Gloria for the rest of the day.

Thanks to Kyle, of course, our mission was one of the best—very neat and colorful and important-looking, because of the clay and the bells. It got a lot of compliments.

That afternoon, Jem Jarrow stayed for an hour and a half. Daddy was somewhere with the truck, getting the carburetor fixed, so he didn't get to see Jem right from the beginning. The first thing Jem did was to work with Ornery George in much the same way that he did the previous Wednesday. Jem was on him within about ten minutes. But then he was off him again. He waved me into the arena. When I got to him, he said, "I forgot to tell you the most important thing."

"What's that?"

"When you're working with an unbroke horse, never be too lazy to get off."

I laughed.

Jem smiled, but then he got serious and looked me in the eye. He said, "I mean it, though. This horse gave me a sign. I felt it. His back is still tense and he's still distracted. Instead of being lazy and thinking that I'll ride him through it, I made up my mind to get off and do a few more things with him before I try him again. Sometimes I don't get on a horse at all during a session. It doesn't do me any good if he hurts me, and it doesn't do him any good, either."

"Daddy says they have to know who's boss. If you get off, then you're giving them their way."

Jem asked George to step over and then step back, then step over the other way, then step forward. George kept looking off toward the gelding corral as if he didn't care one bit about Jem Jarrow, and then Jem raised his hand and made him speed up, and George suddenly tucked his head, curved his body, and looked really beautiful. It was startling. Jem let him come to a halt, and then he gave him a pat. He said to me, "I don't get into a fight with them just to let them know who's boss. Most horses, if they win a fight, it scares them, and if they lose a fight, it makes them resentful."

"After George and my uncle Luke had it out, George was worse."

Jem Jarrow didn't say anything to this. He didn't seem to be an "I-told-you-so" sort of person. After a bit, he got on George again, and this time the horse did all his movements with his ears up and his head and neck relaxed. Also, his hocks were under him, and his response to all of Jem's signals was practically instantaneous. I realized that I had never seen him before without that grumpy look on his face. Jem never let him do the same thing for more than ten or fifteen steps. He turned or halted or cantered or trotted or walked with long steps or made a little circle or figure eight or galloped off and came to a sliding halt or did a neat rotation around his hind feet, first one direction, then the other. He cantered from the halt without bucking.

After they had done all of these things, Jem walked George around, and George continued to look pleased with himself. When they passed me where I was sitting on the fence, I said, "He's a well-trained horse."

Jem said, "He knows a lot of things, yes, but he isn't a well-trained horse until it's his second nature to soften as soon as he's asked to do anything."

"At which point a little girl will be able to ride him."

"I expect a little girl will be able to teach him to do that." He pushed his hat back on his head. He said, "You like that dark one?"

"Yes. That's Black George."

"Well, why don't you go get on him and let's see how he does."

"It's been forty-five minutes."

"Has it? That's fine. Let's try him out."

I put the western tack on Black George, which I hadn't done in a month and a half.

I would have said that Black George was a very good horse. He never bucked or spooked, much less reared or bolted. But after I had taught him, with Jem telling me what to do, to step under in both directions and to drop his nose to the inside and quietly bring his hip around, it was like I was riding a different animal. At the walk, his body was relaxed and loose and I could feel his stride lengthen or shorten every time I asked. At the trot, it was as if the saddle rode his back like a little boat, and I could feel each of his hind legs step under my seat like a little wave. He covered a lot of ground, too. But the canter! The canter wasn't like anything I had ever felt before, rocking and comfortable, but strong and dynamic. I knew that what made it good was right in the shoulder, right in front of my hands. And when I looked at his head, I could just see the bulge of his inside eye; I could also feel his inside hind leg stepping underneath me and launching us, and yet all of these little bits of things I noticed came and went in what seemed like a whoosh of speed. I made small circles and large circles; I asked for a gallop and he leapt forward; I asked for and got a neat halt. The feeling in my stomach had vanished, and school seemed very small and far away. It seemed like I would never make a big deal about anything at school ever again.

Daddy was standing by the fence with Jem. I waved. They talked.

I went over to them. Daddy said, "That looked very nice, young lady."

"He's so comfortable."

"Music to my ears, darling." He shook Jem's hand and walked away.

After Jem left, I tried what he'd taught me on Socks George and the two mares, but what he had taught me, even though I could remember a lot of the very words he had used, was like a refreshing fog that slowly lifted and wafted away. After a while, I had no idea whether I was doing the right thing or not. But he was coming back the very next day. With luck, I thought, Jem might stay two hours.

* * *

In the morning, as soon as we got off the bus, the principal, Mr. Canning, sent us into the lunchroom to have a look at the missions. He and Miss Rowan, the art teacher and Mr. Jarek, the history teacher, stood at the end of the table by San Francisco Solano, smiling and clapping and exclaiming that we had all done a wonderful job, the best ever. The display was more elaborate now—the sixth graders had added some things to the map, just as we had done the year before, when we were in sixth grade—mostly cutouts of cattle and sheep and some fish and whales out in the ocean, as well as two models of sailing ships. The photos of the missions "as they are today" were taped to the wall. Miss Rowan had brought a plate of peanut butter cookies, and we all had one.

Out by the lockers, while we were waiting for the bell, Stella looked happier than she had looked in weeks. And she was also nicer to me. While she was smiling at me and asking how my horses were (she never asked this, normally), her eyes kept drifting toward Brian, Joan, and Mary A., who were talking about bologna sandwiches in loud voices. I said that the horses were fine, and then I said, "Stella, listen to them! Why do you even care?"

"Care about what?"

"About him. Or them. Any of it."

"What makes you think I care?"

"You're looking at them."

"He's just wearing a very strange shirt is all."

He wasn't, though.

At this point, one of the eighth-grade boys walked by, a kid I'd been riding the bus with since kindergarten, named Dougie Wilder. Stella gave him a big smile and said, "Hi, Dougie!"

He looked at her and walked on without saying anything.

I said, "Why do you speak to them?"

"Why not? I'm a friendly person."

"You say hi to them and they don't answer back."

She waved her hand, then she said, "My mom said I could have a party. A boy-girl party. But I have to invite everyone in the class. Can you come?"

"My mom will say yes and my dad will say no, so it depends."

"On what?"

"That's what I don't know."

"Your family is so weird, Abby."

"Well, yeah," is what I said.

"Anyway, if you come, you have to wear something nice" is what she said. She made her voice sound like she was telling me a friendly secret, but I knew she was being mean.

After lunch, when we were at our lockers, Kyle came up to me and said, "You got any glue or Scotch tape or anything like that in your locker?"

I had some Elmer's. I handed it to Kyle. He said, "Some of those trees you made fell over. I'm going to make little stands on the bottom of them. I already colored them brown, but I want to glue them, not just slot them in."

"Okay. But what about your next class?"

"It's gym. I hate gym."

"Don't they care if you're late?"

"Not if you're working on your mission." He took the glue and turned away.

I went to science. We studied barometric pressure. After science, I went back to my locker, thinking solely of showing Jack to Jem Jarrow and finding out how to make him perfect

179

starting right now. I was rummaging around in the bottom of my locker for my colored pencils, and someone bumped me from behind and made me hit my head on the back of the locker. I stood up. Kyle said, "Oh, sorry. I didn't mean to run into you. Here's your glue." He held it out to me, then he said, "I worked on those trees until they were practically growing, waiting for her to go away. She walked all over the place and looked at every mission about six times. I reset the bells. I did everything I could think of."

"What are you talking about?"

"I'm thinking she was going to spill her root beer all over it."

"Who?"

"Your friend Stella. She kept walking around with it and taking tiny little sips and looking over at me, but I didn't look at her, I just kept doing stuff."

"What happened?"

"Well, the bell rang, and then she stood around for a while, and then she left."

We looked at each other. I'm not sure that Kyle and I had ever looked at each other for more than half a second, but now we were both thinking about the same thing, so we looked at each other. Then he said, "But the evidence is only circumstantial."

"What does that mean?"

"It means we could report her only if she really spilled her root beer."

I got that feeling in my stomach again. I said, "What about Gloria? Was she around?"

"No." Then he shrugged. "I did reset the bells. They ring good now."

Jem Jarrow was already there as soon as I got off the bus, and the first thing he said to me was, "Mind if we have a look at the colt?"

Of course not. Jem already had his rope halter out, and he followed me to the pen.

Jack had his head up and his ears pricked, looking right at me. He always did when I came down the road from the school bus. Most of the time, he whinnied or squealed, too. What I did first when I saw him was to pet him on the head and neck, both sides. No treats. Almost every adult in the world that I knew said that treats make a horse nippy, though Daddy would give a trained horse a bit of something once in a while. Sometimes, I picked a handful of grass and let Jack take that between his lips, especially if it was green and moist.

Jem said, "Show me what you do with him."

I went and got the halter and the chamois. Jack stood nicely for putting on the halter. Once he had it on, I started leading him around, and he was okay for the first while, but then he got balky and distracted. I turned him and led him a little bit more. He stopped, threw his head up, and started backing up. Then he came with me again, but when we got back to the gate, I was disappointed and thought that he could have behaved himself better, but then I thought the other thing I always thought, which was that he was just a baby and he would get better as he got older. I held the lead rope with one hand and rubbed the chamois over him with the other, first one side, then the next. He stood quietly for that.

Jem said, "How old is he now?"

"Almost three months."

"He's a big colt."

"He might be a Thoroughbred."

"Looks like it. Why don't you let him go for a minute." This was not a question. When I let him go, he trotted off, his neck arched and his ears pricked. All of a sudden, he reared up a little and pawed, as if he had an imaginary enemy to scare away. He leapt into the air and ran a few strides, then he kicked out. A lot of his foal coat was gone now, and the dark, shiny coat underneath looked sparkly in the sun.

Jem said, "It's going to be a big job, raising this colt."

"That's what everybody says."

"His dam would normally be doing a lot of the work for you."

"I know."

"My suggestion, you turn him out with the geldings."

"I'm afraid he'll get hurt."

"He might, with the mares. Less likely with the geldings, but there's always a risk. First thing, though, he needs to know what they all need to know—how to step over and get out of your space when you ask him to."

Jack had by now come back over to us, his neck arched and his ears pricked, just as interested as he could be. Jem let him be close but not too close. If Jack pressed into him, Jem lifted the halter in his hand and waved it a bit. When Jack then backed up a step, Jem stepped toward him and gave him a pat. Two times, he made the colt back up three or more steps, then he gently touched the side of his face and asked him to turn his head. When his head had turned pretty far, Jack unbent by stepping over. Jem gave him a pat. He said, "One good thing is, if a horse is curious, a colt is twice as curious. If a horse wants to play, and horses do, because otherwise why would they do most of the things we ask them to do, a colt wants to play all the time. Your job is to teach him not to play rough. That's what his dam would do."

I said, "I never thought of what horses do as playing."

"Sure it is. You seen a horse work a cow? That horse is going to tell that cow what to do, pretty much the same as two kids playing tag. My feeling is, the more the horse likes the game, the less the cow does." He smiled and waved Jack away more energetically. First, Jack threw his head up, snorting, and pricked his ears, then he spun and galloped across the pen with his tail curled over his back. After that, he arched his neck and trotted around in a circle, snorting even more loudly and staring at Jem and his rope. He lifted his feet high, then halted again and whinnied. He was tremendously cute. Jem said, "Every move that colt makes, he makes because he enjoys it and it expresses something. He wasn't afraid of the rope when I shook it—he took the shaking of the rope as a reason to move, and then he enjoyed himself moving."

"And we enjoyed watching."

"Well, there you go. Showing, going in parades, working cattle, racing, you name it, if the horses didn't enjoy it, they wouldn't have given humans any ideas about what a horse could do for them."

"Plowing?"

Now Jem really laughed. He said, "Oh, you are something, Miss Abby. You make me laugh. But who says a plow horse doesn't enjoy pulling the plow? How are you going to make him if he doesn't want to do it?"

I was sure that there were ways, and of course, I had read *Black Beauty*, but I liked the way Jem thought of it, so I didn't talk back.

In the meantime, Jack returned to us as if pulled on a rubber band, and this time, Jem put the halter on him while I went and stood outside the gate. Jack acted as if he were a little insulted by the halter and started trotting away, but Jem held on, and Jack came around. Jem waved the end of the rope at him as he got close, and Jack went on past him, pretty soon taking some steps in a circle around Jem but still tossing his head a little. Then, very easily, Jem put some pressure on the rope, and Jack, without even seeming to realize what he was doing, stepped his inside hind leg in front of his outside hind leg and turned smoothly inward. His ears were flicking back and forth. He hesitated. Jem now lifted his left hand, and when Jack moved away from that a little, he found himself going the other way, trotting to the right around Jem's little circle. I saw right away that with a colt even more than with a horse, your job was to give him a little suggestion more than a strict command. If he was playing a game, then you wanted the game to be fun but to also have rules. Jem did this with him for only five minutes or so, just as if it were a game. When Jack was standing quietly, Jem called me over. I opened the gate and closed it behind me.

He handed me the rope and said, "Jake seen the colt?"

"I think he's coming this week."

"Good, because you got to keep a colt's feet in good trim so his feet and legs will develop right. Let's pick his feet up."

"Sometimes I do that when I'm rubbing him down. I rub the chamois down his legs to his feet and then I pick the foot up."

Jem did the same thing, only with his hands—he rubbed from the shoulder downward, down the forearm and then over the knee. When Jack seemed uncomfortable, he stopped his hands moving, but he didn't move away, and then Jack would relax, and Jem would move his hands downward again. He didn't get all the way to his feet at first, just a little closer every time, until after a few tries, he reached a foot and asked Jack to pick it up and stand for a moment on three legs. It was a short moment, though. And then he would drop the foot.

Jem stood up straight and looked at me. He said, "Now, you don't put the foot down. That can be irritating to him. You just let the foot go and he'll stand up on it." He worked his way around the colt, doing this with each foot. I think because of what I'd done with the chamois, Jack didn't mind, really. By the time I did it myself, Jack was standing up like a pro and letting me hold his foot up for maybe thirty seconds. Thirty seconds is a long time when you are holding up a horse's foot and waiting to drop it.

After that, we petted Jack and let him go. Jem said to me, "You've done a good job with him so far, Abby, because he likes you and he lets you be around him. He's half doing what you say because you say it and half doing it because it's interesting to him. That's not bad. But soon he's going to be a big fellow, and you're going to want to rely on him to behave himself—not to get distracted or worked up about things that happen. So you need to work with him every day and give him good habits."

I nodded.

"Let's put him in with the geldings and see what happens."

I must have looked shocked, because he smiled and said, "There's only three of them. If they seem overbearing, we'll grab him and take him out. But he needs to understand other horses, or he'll live a sad life."

I could see this all too well. It was rather like seventh grade.

All we had to do was stand there in order for Jack to come back to us, looking for something, as always. When Jack got to me, I patted him while he snuffled my hands and my hair. Then I slipped the halter on, showing off a little that I could do it smoothly rather than roughly. Then I turned and walked away, and Jack walked along with me toward the gate. Jem said, "Pause, just because you feel like pausing. He should pause, too." He did. But when we went out of the gate, the colt was all eyes. And when he saw that I was leading him toward the gelding pasture, I felt him fill up, sort of like a balloon, and begin to jog. Jem said, "Turn him. He doesn't get to do the most interesting thing unless he can contain himself." As we were passing the hay barn, Jem grabbed a few flakes of hay.

The three geldings were maybe a hundred feet out into the pasture, nibbling grass, but they looked up as soon as they saw us coming, and Socks George threw up his head and gave a whinny. Jack answered. Luckily, though, they just stood there staring as I brought Jack to the gate, and Jem opened it. Jem said, "Pretend there's nothing important going on. Just walk him through the gate and out a ways, and then turn him and get him to lower his head so you can take off the halter." I did.

Jack stood staring at the big horses, his ears pricked, and then, when they came toward him, he started smacking his lips together, which made a little noise. His ears went from being pricked to simply flopping to the side. He dropped his head a little. Jem said, "See what his lips are doing, the way he's showing his teeth a little? He's saying to them, 'I'm a baby.'"

"He never seems to think of himself as a baby."

"Well, he is, and he knows it. And they know it, too, so they expect him to act like a baby."

"What do you mean?"

"Low man on the totem pole."

"Oh."

Now the geldings came over to him, Black George in the lead and the other two right behind him. Then Black George first, Ornery George, and Socks George sniffed noses with him. They sniffed the rest of him while he stood quietly, occasionally flapping his lips. He didn't jump or move or kick out. He tried to sniff their noses, too, but carefully, so as not to cause offense. Ornery George gave him a little bite on the neck. I gasped, but the bite didn't seem mean exactly, more like he was trying it out. Jack flicked his ears backward, but he didn't pin them, as if he were saying, "Okay, bite me if you have to."

Then he made a wrong move, as if he couldn't contain himself and just didn't know what he was doing. He leapt up and struck out with his front hoof. Black George squealed and his ears went back. Jack lowered his head immediately. I said, "They're kind of bossy."

Jem said, "Not really. The three of them, it's more of a club than a dictatorship." We continued to watch, but Jem made no move to go in or rescue him.

As for me, I did want him to fit into the club, but I knew that the club could change—would change, if Daddy had his way, and that the members of the club could get meaner. One thing I loved about Jack, and one of the reasons that I watched him sometimes, was that he didn't know what the rules were. He ran, he leapt, he snorted, he stared at geckos and ground squirrels, he pawed things and investigated. He whinnied and squealed and came running, or went running. He was willing to try anything out, and he looked beautiful doing it. His neck arched, his feet lifted, his tail went up, his nostrils flared. A breeze might get him going, or a bird taking off from a branch, or the sight of the other horses galloping. He was by himself, so he had to make his own fun, and we all knew that the fun that kids sometimes make for themselves isn't that good for them. Still, he was the only creature on the place who did what he wanted to when he wanted to do it. I liked watching.

Jem said, "Well, it's going pretty well, I think."

Black George seemed to lose interest. He walked away. The others followed. Jack stood there, then he followed.

Jem said, "If he follows, he's saying that they are the bosses. And that's what we want him to say. The bosses pretend not to notice the underlings, and the underlings show that they are always aware of the bosses. That's how horse herds work. So you watch for a bit. You'll see that now they will all pretend to ignore him, but they'll test him a little bit to see if he's paying attention." And it was true—just a bit after Jem said that,

Socks George trotted past Jack, kind of close to him, in fact, without seeming to notice him, and Jack stepped back to let him go by and then turned toward him. Jem said, "The chestnut just showed who was boss, and Jack just showed that he understands that."

I said, "What if they gang up on him—"

"My thought is that these horses aren't going to do that. They're pretty consistent, and they have a pretty stable group—"

"Club."

"Yeah. I don't think they'll kick him—that's why I didn't put him in with the mares. Mares kick more than geldings. He looks like he knows his place. That's not to say that later he won't decide that he isn't a baby anymore. But he knows he's a baby now, and they will remind him of that fact with a nip here and there, so don't be surprised if you come out and find a few bites on him." He turned and looked at me. He said, "The geldings are doing a job that you would have to do, Abby. It's a job that has to be done, especially with a bright colt like this fellow."

"Like school."

"Like school."

He said, "Okay, now let's give everyone some hay. It's almost feeding time, and at feeding time, horses get a little worried. Once they all have plenty of hay and the colt doesn't bother them at theirs, then everyone will settle down."

We set out five piles. Jack started out at the farthest-away pile, mouthing the hay and eating a little. Then he moved to the next one closest to the other geldings. Ornery George looked at him once and flicked his ears backward, but then they all settled to eating, and I let out that long breath I had been holding.

189

Western Saddle

Western Stirrups

Farrier's Apron

Chapter 15

Jem left shortly after that, and I felt his reassurance all through supper and all through my homework (and anyway, I went out to check on the geldings two or three times before I went to bed). After she fed Jack his bran mixture, Mom came in and told me they would be all right, and Daddy said that if I was worried, then I should turn it over to the Lord, because then the best thing would happen. I nodded, but we both knew that the "best thing" could always be a trial of some sort, which I frankly didn't think I was ready for. But even in the morning everyone was fine. I got up early and watched them before school. I saw that Jack did his romping and playing a little off by himself, but the geldings watched him with pricked ears, like indulgent uncles. He watched them, too. When they got their hay and settled down to eat it, he stood in the line like they did, switching his little tail (I always set the hay piles out in a long line, each pile about ten feet from the others). Perfectly relaxed.

But I was so tired from waking up in the night and worrying about him that I fell asleep on the school bus, which I would have thought was an impossible thing to do. When we got to school, I woke up, but I was sleepy all through homeroom and first period. And it wasn't until I went to the girls' bathroom during the break that I realized what I looked like. My hair was flat on one side and sticking out on the other side and my blouse was wrinkled, too, because I had picked it out of my closet without really looking at it in the dark. What a mess. No wonder Stella wanted to make sure I would wear something nice to her party.

By lunch, I had more or less fixed myself. At least Stella and Gloria didn't say anything. They were talking about the mission open house and potluck that night. Gloria's mom was going to bring steamed artichokes with a special sauce and Stella's mom was going to bring the safest thing, chocolate chip cookies. Stella told Gloria that her mom was weird and Gloria shrugged, as if to say, Well, we all know that. Then Stella got up to go to the girls' bathroom to do something, and even though I expected Gloria to follow her, she didn't. She leaned toward me and said, "Guess what?"

"What?"

"Remember that ink thing? When Joan got the ink on her skirt?"

I sat very still and said, "Yeah, sure."

"Somebody sent Joan an anonymous note and said it was Stella, that she did it on purpose with the cartridge from her pen, and Joan's mom showed the note to Mr. Canning."

I decided to be very careful. I said, "Do you think Stella did that? It's a really mean thing to do."

"Ha!" exclaimed Gloria, tossing her head. "I bet Joan wrote the note herself and sent it to herself, then showed it to her mom to blame it on Stella. That's what I think. I wouldn't put it past her."

She sounded like she believed that, but really, I didn't feel like I could figure anything out anymore. I said, "Don't you think things were easier before Stella came into our class?"

Gloria shrugged. She said, "Not as fun, though. More boring." We got up, put away our trays, and went into study hall. While I did my work, I thought about the fact that Jem Jones would be coming for one more day, on Saturday. It seemed like a treasure to know that.

Everything was normal that night, which was a Wednesday. We went to our chapel, and I gave thanks that I didn't have to talk to Daddy about the missions and whether I had witnessed to Kyle and the other kids about the wrongful history of the Catholic Church and all of that. That Wednesday, we happened to sing a lot. Daddy sang one of my favorites, one called "Deep River," that he didn't sing much. Then Mr. Hazen sang one called "Lonely Road" that I hadn't heard before. And we all sang all the verses of "Amazing Grace," including the one about the earth dissolving like snow. On the way home in the car, Daddy and Mom did a duet of "How Can I Keep from Singing?" which is one of my favorites of all time. When we checked on the horses before going to bed, everyone was quiet and happy, and Black George was standing by Jack, as if he had decided the colt was his boy.

No one was happy when I got to school in the morning, though. The Big Four were gathered around Joan's locker, gossiping in low tones, Brian Connelly was absent, and Stella and Gloria didn't have much to say. I went to algebra, then we had assembly, and in assembly, I found out what was wrong. Joan had worn her add-a-pearl necklace to the potluck. It had thirteen pearls on it and was very valuable, though Mr. Canning didn't say how much it was worth. Joan had been careless with the necklace, Mr. Canning admitted that—she hadn't noticed until she was in the girls' bathroom that it was no longer around her neck. Everyone had looked high and low. The necklace could not be found, and so it could only be assumed that someone had picked it up. That someone was expected to turn it in. Once again, I was glad I hadn't gone to the potluck.

For lunch, I had a sandwich made of a slice of the pot roast Mom had made for the prayer meeting. That was good, too.

Gloria and Stella agreed that they couldn't figure out why that necklace was such a big deal. Joan, of course, said they were real pearls rather than cultured pearls, but whose mother would let her wear real pearls to a potluck? And heels. Joan had also worn heels—two inch. "It was a potluck!" said Stella. "Why be overdressed? It's much worse to be overdressed than under-dressed for a party. My mom says that's practically a law."

Gloria nodded as if, in spite of the red boots and cowboy shirts and all, she understood this law perfectly.

This went on for all day Thursday. Joan's mother even came Thursday afternoon—I saw her enter the building and then go into the principal's office. But, to be perfectly frank, since I hadn't been at the potluck, I didn't think it was any of my business. When I got home Thursday afternoon, it didn't even occur to me to tell Mom about it, and if it had occurred to me, then I would have had to tell her about the missions, so I wouldn't have told her anyway.

Maybe because of the nice service we had had, Daddy was in a good mood all of Thursday and Friday morning. He helped me with everything, whistled a few tunes, ruffled my hair. And the weather was good. When we got up in the morning, it was already light. We had gotten past Mom's daffodils and well into the tulips, and even the irises were starting to bud out. Jack wandered around with the geldings as if he had been living with them for years. He spent most of his time not far from Black George, and they made a beautiful pair when they pricked their ears and trotted around. Black George was only four, actually, so he seemed to remember what it was like to be a colt. He and Jack would lift their tails and trot big and snort or pretend that crows taking off from the fence rail were exciting and run off leaping and kicking. Socks George and Ornery George didn't play with them much, but once in a while for a few moments they would pick up a gallop and take off across the pasture.

By Friday afternoon, the necklace thing was a big deal. In a special assembly, Mr. Canning told us in his sternest voice that Joan's parents were very upset, and that the sheriff knew about it, and that there would be repercussions if the person or persons who had the necklace did not come forward "of his or her own accord." I, of course, had my suspicions, but I didn't tell them to anyone, especially not Gloria and, when I got home, especially not Mom. Mom was a complete believer in "coming forward" because it was "in the end the kindest thing to do" and "a form of witnessing." But in seventh grade, a person who came forward was known as a snitch, and that would be the end of that person.

On Saturday morning, another beautiful day, I was up and dressed to ride by seven. Jem Jarrow appeared during breakfast. Mom asked if he would like some pancakes, which is what we were having, but he settled for a glass of water and drank it on the front porch. I gobbled down my pancakes and went out.

As we walked to the gelding paddock, he said, "You seem ready to go, Abby."

"I am. I couldn't wait for today."

He smiled. He said, "Horses are like that, too, you know. If you finish the lesson with a horse wanting to do more of what you want to teach him, he'll always be happy in his work."

The first horse we tacked up was Black George. While we were cleaning him and putting the English saddle and bridle on him, Jack stood at the gate, ears pricked, watching us. After I had mounted and we were walking toward the arena, Jem said, "That's good. That means he's got a friend."

"Black George is pretty nice with him. He plays a little."

"He's a good-natured fella."

"Daddy says he could be a show horse."

Jem didn't say anything, but not in a way that meant he disagreed, just in a way that meant it wasn't his place to have an opinion on that. We went into the arena.

196

I did everything Jem told me to do, in order—stepping over several times on each side until Black George was really moving along, loose and agreeable, but full of energy, too. Then I asked him to halt and then go forward a few times. Jem said I was to try and feel which leg was stepping forward first when I asked him to walk, and pretty soon I could feel that it was one of the hind legs, which meant that his whole body moved at the same time—if a front leg goes first, then the hind legs get left behind, but if a hind leg goes first, then it pushes the whole body ahead of it, and everything keeps together. Halt to walk, walk to trot, halt to trot. Black George felt springy and happy, not to mention comfortable. Then I did some work at the trot—trotting forward, holding back, turning in loops and circles. Black George kept his neck arched and his mouth soft—all I had to do to change the speed or direction was to twitch the reins, and he did what was asked. When we cantered, it was like silk.

When we were finished, Jem said, "That's the easy one. That's the one I want you to think about when you're riding the hard one. You were riding English, so I'll tell you a story. I was training a horse last year, a big Thoroughbred, an old racehorse with lots of experience. Not an educated horse in some ways. We were loping, and I started thinking a thought, and the thought was that there was an elastic band attaching my elbow to his hocks, easy and soft but keeping us together in the best way possible. And while I was thinking that thought, I asked that horse to pivot. Now, this was a big horse, seventeen hands, and long, too. But when I turned him, thinking that thought, he did a perfect pivot, da dum, da dum, da dum, a hundred and eighty degrees, and off in the other direction.

"I also knew a fella who showed up early at the barn out on the coast to try a bay horse over some jumps. So he tacks her up, gets on her, takes her out in the ring, and jumps the course easy as you please. When he gets back to the barn, he finds out he was on the wrong bay horse—not the fancy jumper he meant to buy, but a three-year-old just off the track not more than a week. Never jumped a fence in her life. Now what am I telling you?"

"That all my wishes will come true?"

"Yes, Abby, but more importantly than that, if you have a real feeling in your mind of what you want the horse to do, your own body will communicate to the horse how to do it. This is a good, athletic, and cooperative horse. The feeling he gives you is the one you want from the others."

"So my main job is to remember that feeling?"

"I would say so, yes."

When we put Black George back into the paddock, Jack came over to meet him, and they trotted around for a moment, kicking up. Then they settled to the same pile of oat hay.

We saddled up Ornery George, and then I went to put on the bridle, but Jem stopped me. He motioned toward Jack's empty pen, and I saw that I had to start with the groundwork. I made myself remember what Jem had done earlier in the week—lead him on a loose line, don't let him crowd me, stop suddenly and then move on, lift the end of the rope and insist that he back off. Jem said, "He's actually not a terribly ill-mannered horse, but he's a little ill-mannered. You need to ask him to do it really right, not sort of right."

It took us ten minutes to walk over to the pen, because I

tried to correct George every time he did a wrong thing, but when we got there, George might as well have been heeling and sitting like a dog, he was paying attention that well.

I stood in the center and sent him around me, to the left and the right. When he did what he wanted to do, I made him do more of it until he wanted to stop, and then I made him do what I wanted him to do. He tossed his head and switched his tail, but only a few times. After a while—say, by the time we were both sweating—his ears were flopped and his eye was soft. He was moving his shoulder away from me whenever I asked him to, and that made his body as soft as could be.

I got on.

I did from the saddle just what I had been doing from the ground, all the time trying to keep the Black George feel. It wasn't easy. Ornery George was stiffer and less springy than Black George. Whereas Black George could go all the way around the circle without stiffening, Ornery George could only go three or four strides, but three or four strides was enough. Once I got the feel of those, I could get him to do it for five, and then six, and then back the other way. I was busy. He was busy. I realized that he wasn't thinking about bucking, and then I realized that I wasn't thinking about him bucking—I was too busy thinking about other things that I wanted him to do.

When I was a little out of breath, I halted him, and Jem called out to me to ride him over to the arena. He was fine in the bigger space, too. Finally, I asked for the lope, and off we went, rocking back and forth, not terribly fast, but going where we wanted to go. Jem motioned with his hand, and I turned Ornery George on a circle and brought him to a halt.

Then we trotted off again, the other direction, and did the canter, just a few strides, again. We cantered halfway around the arena, and then Jem motioned me to the middle. I did that circle again, but in the other direction, and came to a halt. Jem said, "That's enough, I think. Stop while it's still fresh in your mind . . ."

"Just one more canter?"

He grinned—the first real grin that I'd ever seen—and said, "Do you think he would like that?"

"Yes."

"Save it for tomorrow. He'll have something to look forward to. Your assignment for today is very small."

"What is it?"

"Remember what you felt this morning on these two horses."

"I will."

"And get off now and walk him out so nothing gets in the way of that."

I was off in two seconds. George gave me a look of surprise. I'd been on him maybe twenty minutes, but I knew without Jem telling me that a good twenty minutes was plenty.

At lunch, Daddy said, "I was watching you. You looked good."

I had been concentrating so hard, I hadn't even seen him.

The next day, at our chapel, those Greeley kids sat still for half an hour, through four straight readings of *The Little Engine That Could*, and then the baby fell asleep and slept for the rest of the afternoon. We had strawberry shortcake, the cake kind, with whipped cream, and we really did give thanks.

* * *

Monday morning was rainy and cold, and I had to admit to Mom that I'd left my heavy sweater at school. She suggested that the fact that I was shivering inside my raincoat was something I would think about the next time I didn't bother to bring home my sweater.

The bus was late, and there was a bit of a crush at my end of the lockers. My raincoat was wet, and Joan said, "Ugh," as I pressed past her. I said, "Sorry, it's really raining," as if she didn't know that. She looked at me and wiped her hand across her skirt to get the rain off.

Stella said, "Were the bus windows open or something?" And then I took the lock off my locker and opened the door. The first thing I saw was my sweater, navy blue, right where I'd left it, and the next thing I saw was a string or something, and then Joan said, "Hey!"

And Stella said, "Oh, wow!"

And Mary A. said, "There's Joan's necklace!"

She dove for it, then held it up, and then Joan grabbed it out of her hand. The two of them ran down the hall.

This didn't take more than a couple of moments. Stella said, "Oh, Abby! Now what? You'll be in so much trouble."

"For what?"

"That's the necklace!"

"I never saw that necklace before. I didn't even know what it was. I thought it was a piece of string."

Then the bell rang. I put on my sweater, even though I wasn't cold anymore. I walked slowly to algebra, and when I went through the door, the Big Four gave me four big dirty looks.

I suppose some kids would have gone up to the Big Four

and declared right there that they had never seen the necklace and hadn't taken the necklace, but I didn't think of that. I just sat in my seat all through algebra going back and forth between wondering how the necklace got into my locker, since it was locked, and wondering what kind of trouble I was in. I couldn't really think straight, because it was all such a mystery. It's very hard to go from being the last person in the world to find out about something to the person everyone is sure did that thing. It made me stupid (I couldn't answer any of Mr. Jepsen's questions), and it gave me a headache. I kept looking at my sweater in a dumb way, as if something about it would tell me how the necklace got there. I knew I had left the sweater in my locker on Thursday around lunch, noticed it a few times after that, forgotten it Thursday afternoon, and forgotten it again Friday. I hadn't hung it up on the hook, because Mom said sweaters were to be folded, not hung, so a book or two had been on top of it once in a while. I should have folded it and set it on the upper shelf, but then—These were the thoughts I kept thinking, but I just couldn't make it out.

In the middle of second period, I was called out of social studies to the principal's office. As soon as I went in there, I saw the necklace on Mr. Canning's desk, and then he said, "Well, Abby, I'm very disappointed in you."

I didn't say anything.

"What do you have to say about this?"

I didn't say anything, then I said, "I don't know."

"Since I wasn't there this morning, I have to ask you, Abby, whether this necklace was found in your locker?"

I nodded.

"How did it get there?"

"I don't know."

He shook his head. He said, "I am going to ask you again, Abby, how did the necklace get into your locked locker?"

"I don't know."

"Does someone else know the combination to your lock?"

"I don't know. I don't think so."

"Well, that leaves you up a crick, doesn't it?"

"Yes, sir."

"I'm going to ask you again how the necklace got into your locker."

"I don't know, Mr. Canning. I didn't even go to the potluck."

"Well, Abby, we do know that the necklace was lost at the potluck, but we don't know that it was found at the potluck."

I said, "Yes, sir."

"I have called your mother."

I didn't say anything.

"I'm sorry you've decided to be obdurate on this, even if you are protecting someone else. But it is a valuable necklace, and everyone in school was warned about keeping it quiet and everyone was asked to come forward, so everyone has had a chance to be honest."

I stood there.

"Do you understand what I mean?"

"Yes, sir."

What was I thinking through all this? I don't know. I was looking at the shelves behind Mr. Canning's desk and at the stuff on his desk (a small stuffed bear because he went to UCLA, a picture of his son in a football uniform, a picture of his dog). Mostly I was scared, and it didn't make me less scared that Mom was on her way to school. I didn't for a moment think that Mom would think I stole the necklace, but I did think she would make a fuss about the missions. Mr. Canning said, "Well, Abby. I was hoping you would be more forthcoming. I'm disappointed."

I said, "Yes, sir."

"You may go now." I went out of his office.

The bell rang and it was time for English, but instead I went out onto the steps and waited until our car drove up to the door. I could hear Mom talking even before I could see her, saying, "—and what could all this about suspension possibly mean? I don't understand a word of this! I can't believe you've left me in such ignorance, young lady! What are the missions?"

"Please don't talk to him about the missions."

"What are the missions?"

"It's a school project where we learn about the California missions, and everyone has to build one, so I—"

"You built a Catholic mission?"

"We all did."

"Daniel did not."

"I'm sure he did, Mom. If you ask him."

But by now we were at the door of the principal's office. We knocked and walked in.

Mr. Canning said what he had to say, which was that a valuable necklace had been taken and hidden and then found in my locker, but I was not revealing anything about it, either because I had taken it or because I was "protecting a friend very unwisely."

And Mom said what she had to say, which was that I could not have possibly taken the necklace and it was highly unlikely that I would protect anyone, because I was a good girl and a well-taught girl and I would certainly come forward if I had any knowledge, so there was something going on, no doubt about that, and what was this about Catholic missions?

Mr. Canning explained that the misson project was a universal history project in California schools. State law.

"Never heard of it before. My son, Daniel—"

"Daniel and his partner built a very nice mission, as I remember. Was it cut-up cardboard boxes? Colorful and nicely painted. Mission San Miguel, I think." He sighed and looked down.

Mom stared at him.

The only thing they agreed on was that I would be suspended for some days or at least until the school got to the bottom of the necklace mystery.

We walked to the car, and Mom said that we would talk about it later, after she had calmed down. That was okay with me. I looked at the hall clock as we were leaving the school. Two hours had passed since the first bell, and I was leaving already. Mom walked in front of me as we headed toward the car, which was parked at the far end of the parking lot. Her shoes made a sharp thudding noise on the tarmac, and even the back of her head and her shoulders looked mad. I wondered if I could remember the last time Mom had gotten mad—usually that was Daddy's department. I tried to imagine what would happen next and what I would do about it, but I couldn't.

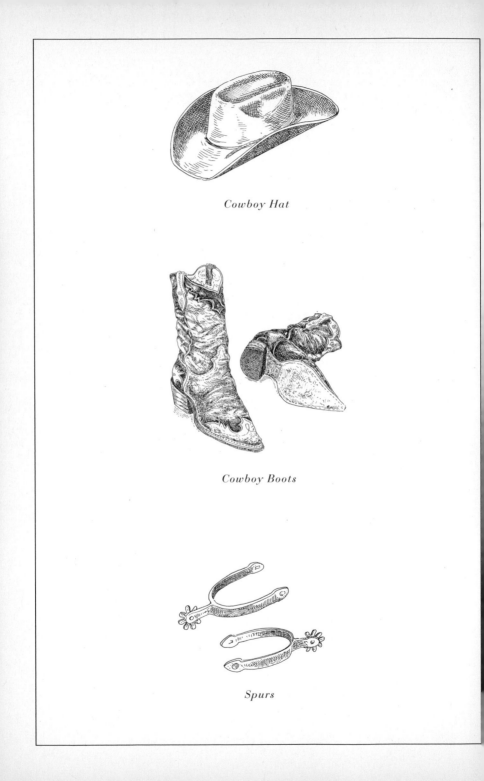

Cowboy Hat

Cowboy Boots

Spurs

Chapter 16

WE GOT HOME BEFORE LUNCHTIME. DADDY'S TRUCK WAS gone, which was probably a good thing. I decided to get all my horse work done, but after I had put my jeans on and gone out to the barn, I began to wonder what the point of it all was. The horses looked happy in their pastures. The three mares were standing in a straggling line on the brow of the hill, dark in the noon sunshine. Their pasture was big enough to still have some grass, and one of the mares was grazing, but the other two were standing ears to tail not far from the biggest oak tree, their heads down, idly switching flies. In the gelding pasture, I didn't see Jack for a moment, and then I saw him lying flat out, asleep in the sunlight. Black George was grazing about halfway between him and the other two. Ornery George was methodically licking the bottom of a bucket that was tied to the fence—Jack's bucket, in which Mom had probably fed him his morning mixture of bran and milk—and Socks George was over by the water trough, pushing his nose into the water, then shaking his head, then pawing the ground with his left front hoof. He did this three times, and even though I knew that Daddy didn't like the horses playing in the water, he looked like he was having fun.

I stood there, and I have to say that I didn't know what in the world to do. I wasn't used to having Mom mad at me, I knew that Stella wasn't my friend anymore, and that only left Gloria. But Gloria was lost, too—without even realizing it at the time, I had noticed Gloria that morning, and now that came back to me. Just after Stella saw the necklace, Gloria, who was standing behind her, didn't look shocked or upset, she just turned away for a moment and then looked back, like a person staring in a crowd, not like the best friend you've had for your whole life. She looked, in fact, like she didn't care. I realized that she was going to use what happened as a way to drop me without having a fight or saying anything at all. I looked back at the house. I couldn't see Mom anywhere, so I opened the mares' gate, closed it behind me, and headed down to the crick. I skirted way around the mares so as not to bother them. Blue Jewel turned her head and looked at me, but no one moved. I headed down the hill. The oaks along the crick looked inviting—shady dark green in the damp grass—so I headed there.

The crick was sometimes high and mostly low. This time of year, the water ran over the stones, not through them, but, except in one pool, it wasn't more than six inches deep. It was pretty, though, shining, clear, and ripply, making wrinkles and rivulets over all the stones. The shadows of the leafy branches above danced over the water, and the grass, long and moist, draped over the banks. The sand along the bottom of the pool was gray and rough—not like beach sand. The water in the pool was about a foot and a half deep. I threw a few pebbles into it, skipping them the way Danny had taught me, but the pool was wide enough only for one skip. Then I took off my boots and socks and rolled up my jeans. The rocks were slippery to get to the pool, and then the water in the pool was cold. I dug my toes into the gray sand, which felt good, and then wiggled them to go deeper. It was all too easy to imagine having no friends at school ever again. That was the difference, I realized, between one real friend and none. Your one friend surrounded you and made you feel like everything was normal so that you never even thought about the fact that there was only one. But when she was gone, you were stuck with the truth.

I swished around in the pool until my whole body was cold, and then I walked up onto the bank in a sandy part. The sand was sunny and warm, which felt good on my cold feet. Then I went over to one of the trees and sat down on a lower branch where it dipped away from the trunk and then grew upward. It was a thick branch and didn't even bend with my weight. I turned a little and leaned my back against the trunk. I could hear the breeze ruffle through the upper leaves. I closed my eyes. There were lots of noises, but they were all low ones—skittering in the grass, creaking in the tree, indistinguishable wind sounds. Silence.

When I woke up, the mares were practically on top of me, or so it seemed the first moment. But they weren't really. Really, they were just standing in front of me, Blue Jewel in front of the others, her nose about two inches from my knee, Star Jewel next to her, maybe a foot back, and Roan Jewel behind them but with her head up and her ears pricked, like a person trying to see in a crowd. I yawned a couple of times, the way you do when you've been asleep, and Blue Jewel stuck out her nose and sniffed my hands, which were crossed in my lap. Then she nosed my leg. Instead of saying, "No treats," which is what I usually said when they poked around my hands and pockets, I said, "I'm all right."

Star Jewel blew out of her nostrils, as if to say, "Okay, then." I laughed. Roan Jewel then whinnied, and there was something uncanny about the whole thing. I lifted my hand and petted Blue Jewel on the nose, then down the face. She took a half step closer. I put out my other hand and then stroked her around the eyes on both sides, starting up by her cowlick, then stroking outward and downward over her cheeks. She stretched her head out, flopped her ears, and sighed. Then I sighed. The other two came closer. Star Jewel sniffed my jeans and then lowered her head and sniffed my foot. I put my fingers in the mane hair just behind her ears and tickled. She cocked her head as if she was enjoying it. Then Roan Jewel had a thought. While I was petting the others, she went around the tree and came behind me and snuffled the back of my neck and my shirt. Her breath was warm and made my hair lift. I was surrounded.

I knew I could wave them off. I knew I *should* wave them off. At the very least, horses are so unpredictable that a squirrel or a snake suddenly spooking them could make them forget where I was completely in their rush to get away. And I was barefoot—my boots were on the bank fifteen feet away. But I didn't move. I petted them and tickled them and let them sniff me all over, ruffling my hair, investigating my hands, poking their noses under my ear, pushing lightly against me. And then Blue Jewel did an odd thing—she began to lick my shirt, right under my collarbone and over my shoulder. She licked and licked, long after any flavors I would have thought were there would have been licked away. Then she moved up to my neck, then my chin and cheek. Her licks were firm and moist, but not hard or pushy. I realized that this was what it must be like to be a foal and to have your dam lick you.

The other two mares seemed to watch Blue Jewel do her licking—their ears were forward, as if they were saying, "Why is she doing that?" But they didn't mind it. We all relaxed. After she had licked me to her heart's content, Blue Jewel sighed a deep sigh. Roan Jewel had already given up on the back of my neck and now went down into the crick for a drink from the pool. Then the two others followed her. I watched them for a moment, then fetched my boots and socks and put them on.

At the house, Daddy's truck was parked next to the car and the door was closed. I got the halter and long lead rope out of the barn and went to the gate of the gelding pasture. Jack was up by now, and he came right to the gate with a nicker. I wasn't thinking those thoughts about school or Gloria anymore. School seemed quite far away. I knew I would have to think about it later, so why think about it now?

Jack and I went into his old pen and I closed the gate behind us. I walked to the middle and stood there long enough to think about each thing that Jem would want me to do with Jack—make him go around me, make him step over, make him back up, make him go around me the other direction, make him turn his head and neck and soften them, make him relax his neck and put his head down, make him curve his body away from me as he did each movement. Then I asked him to do all those things, and he did them nicely, for no more than fifteen minutes, if that. When we were finished, I got him to stand while I ran the chamois over him from ears to tail, then I picked up his feet, one by one. He made it all seem as though nothing was a big deal. I left him in that pen while I worked with Black George.

The mares came up the hill. One by one, I made my way through all of them, grooming them, picking their feet, tacking them up, taking them to the arena. Then I moved to the geldings. I made sure to begin Ornery George with some groundwork in Jack's pen, but that was the only difference. I had saved him for last, so it was almost suppertime when I was starting with him. Since there was no one around to tell me what to do, I worked at my own speed, but steadily. When I brushed the horses and picked out their feet, I thought about how all of the new horses had gotten better-looking since coming from Oklahoma—shinier and sleeker, with their manes combed and their feet neatly trimmed. Ornery George himself looked as good as I had ever seen him, so I spent some extra time brushing his white points.

When I led him into the pen, he neither pulled nor lagged back, but just walked along with me. Nor was he giving me any looks—he was looking where we were going. I thought, right then, that we were ready. But when I opened the gate, he moved past me as if he didn't care about me, and when I gave the halter rope a jerk and said, "Hey! Pay attention to me, George," he was still oblivious. My heart sank. I thought, Thirty-six dollars down the drain. Something more I would have to talk about with Daddy.

Afterward, I wasn't quite sure why I did what I next did, but what I did was to unclip the halter rope and let him go. When he moved away from me, I swung the rope, and he began to trot around the periphery of the pen, his tail up and his ears pricked, not like he was in a bad mood, but like he was in a good mood. I shook the rope. He bucked and kicked out, then started to gallop. I shook the rope again. He bucked and kicked out again. But he went around me at a safe distance. After two circuits of the pen, I stepped over to my right, just to try it, and Ornery George turned toward me, then went the other direction, bucking and kicking. I then made a little mistake and stepped sort of in front of him—not in front of him literally, but in front of his gaze, even though I was still in the middle of the pen. He slid to the halt, spun, and went back the other direction. It was like we were playing a game, so I kept playing, stepping to the right or the left or toward him, just to see what he would do. He didn't always do anything, but sometimes he did— speeding up, spinning, sliding to a halt and going the other direction. I realized that he was watching me and his moves were reactions to me. Finally, after about ten minutes of this activity, he turned toward me and stopped, and when I stepped toward him, he stepped backward, two neat steps, made as if he meant them. I turned my back and stepped. I heard him come up behind me and felt his breath on my arm. It was as if he were saying, "Time to go for a ride."

I believed him.

Our ride wasn't that big of a deal. We walked, trotted, cantered, halted, backed, made some large, medium-sized, and small circles in both directions, trotted from the halt, halted from the trot, stood quietly for a while while I rested my hand on his haunches. He sighed. No big deal.

That was why it was a big deal.

I walked him out. When I got back to the barn, Daddy was finishing up the evening work. He had filled all the water buckets and put out all the hay, hung up all the tack, and put away the bridles. Without saying anything, he helped me untack Ornery George and brush him off, then put him away. The very fact that he wasn't saying anything let me know that while he appreciated my efforts, there were things to talk about—things that required a family meeting and praying to the Lord for guidance, things that were much too serious to talk about as we were making our way from the barn to the house. The horses had sort of lulled me, hadn't they? But now my stomach started to hurt.

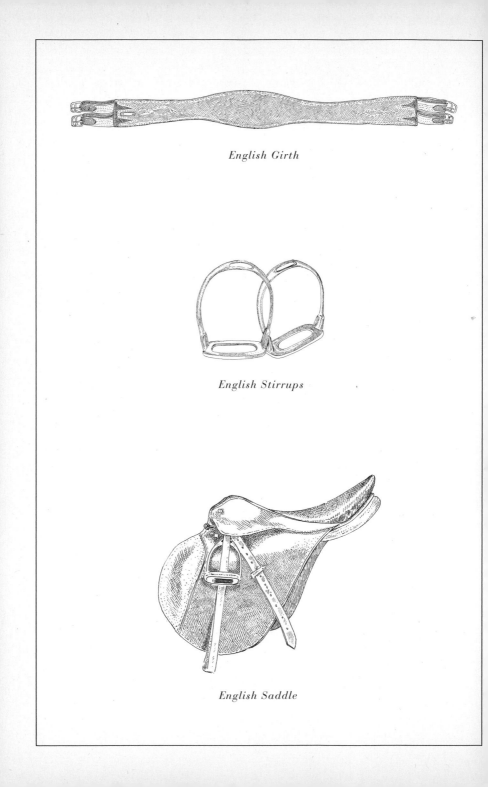

English Girth

English Stirrups

English Saddle

Chapter 17

IT DIDN'T OFTEN HAPPEN IN OUR HOUSE THAT MOM AND DADDY had a quiet conversation over supper. Usually Daddy was excited about something and Mom went along with it, whether it was a good thing or a bad thing. Sometimes, supper was lively and funny, with lots of jokes and a song or two. Other times, supper was loud and not funny at all, because Daddy was righteously angry or resolute in his determination or dedicated to rectifying evil. All the Lovitts were big talkers. But our supper that night was much more like a supper at Gloria's house, where Gloria's mom kept up a steady, soothing patter and Gloria's dad ate first the vegetable, then the meat, then the starch, never letting any one of those touch any of the others. Gloria's house was very neat—even the fringes of the rugs looked like they were combed out straight. We had spaghetti. Thinking again about Gloria, I didn't eat much.

I noticed that our house was very neat, too. That's what Daddy and Mom had been doing while I was out with the horses—turning over a new leaf. In our house, a new leaf always started with the vacuum cleaner and ended up with me going to bed at nine on the dot.

After supper, Daddy went to his desk in the living room, opened his Bible at random, and read a verse. The verse was, "And a certain man found him, and, behold, he was wandering in the field: and the man asked him, saying, What seekest thou?" I saw Mom purse her lips a little and sigh. There was a long pause, and I knew they were trying to figure out what to make of this verse. I said, "I guess they were seeking Joan's necklace for about four or five days." I tried to sound helpful.

Daddy said, "Tell me about this necklace."

I said, "It's an add-a-pearl. Every year on her birthday, her grandmother gives her a pearl, and they string it on with the rest of them."

"So there are twelve pearls?"

"Thirteen. I guess there was one to grow on."

"How valuable would a necklace like that be?"

I shrugged.

Mom said, "At least a hundred dollars. Maybe more depending on the chain and the pearls."

I said, "I didn't take the necklace."

"We don't think you did, honey," said Mom.

I looked at Daddy. He said, "But when the evidence is against you, it's hard to prove a negative. It looks to me like if they suspended you, they feel they've got a pretty good circumstantial case. How could the necklace have gotten into your locker?"

"I don't know, unless somebody knows the combination to my lock. But I haven't told it even to Gloria. They would have to be watching me open it."

"That could be anyone," said Daddy.

We listened to the clock tick for a while, then Daddy said, "I see we are at the mercy of the Lord. May his mercy be upon us."

Mom said, "Amen."

Daddy said, "Now, Abby, you have kept from us this mission-building project, and I wonder if I have been remiss in explaining to you certain facts about the Roman Catholic Church."

I said, "I don't know."

"The thing is, the Roman Catholic Church is a great and powerful enemy. *Our* great and powerful enemy. It has done many things over the centuries to our people and to its own people that are not easy to speak about."

"It was a school assignment. Danny had to do it, too."

"Reminding me that your brother may have been sneaking around behind my back does not make me happier that you have been doing the same thing."

I bit my lips and tried to think of something. I looked at Mom, but it was clear she wasn't going to help me. I knew I was right on the edge between asking a question and sassing back. Daddy didn't seem mad so far, but he could get there in no time. I kept my mouth shut, and he did what he always did, which was to expand on his previous statement. This could be dangerous, too. He said, "Who helped you with this project?"

"Kyle Gonzalez. We made it out of clay, but we didn't fire it. We just let it dry and then painted it."

"Did this boy who has a Mexican name and therefore is probably Roman Catholic witness to you while you were working together?"

"He told me who the missions were named for. Saints. Things like that."

"Which was your mission?"

"San Juan Bautista."

"John the Baptist."

"Yeah."

"At least he's in the Bible," said Mom. "He himself wasn't Roman Catholic like Francis of Assisi or Agnes. You could have ended up with someone else, a real Roman Catholic. Abby, you—"

I said, "Danny did San Miguel. That's the archangel Michael."

They looked at me a moment, letting this remark pass, then Daddy continued, "You need to ask us how to walk this narrow path."

They had been talking for sure. They were a united front. I said, "What should I ask you?" hoping this didn't sound sassy.

Daddy said, "I think I have to go to the school. I think I have to go personally to the school and look over the curriculum and discuss what Abby will be allowed to study and what she won't be allowed to study."

Mom nodded.

My heart sank. I loved my family. Both Daddy and Mom made the other parents I knew look stiff and sad. Everything they did, they did all out. There was never a moment when Daddy didn't mean what he said and say what he meant—most of the time he said what he meant until you couldn't stand to hear it anymore. Mom was prettier and more fun than any other mother—she was prettier and more fun than I was, in fact. But the idea of Daddy and Mom and Mr. Canning and my other teachers never seeing eye to eye was terrifying, because Daddy would keep after them and after them. He didn't know how to stop because he didn't think it was right to stop. He would certainly bring his Bible to school and lay it on Mr. Canning's desk and quote from it every chance he got. I wondered if it might be better, after all, just to get expelled. I could do that if I confessed to stealing the necklace.

Daddy said, "Why don't you bring your books down, Abby, and let me have a look at them. I've been remiss, I see." He sighed.

I got up and went to my room. After putting the books on his desk, I went out to check the horses. Everyone was fine. Blue Jewel was lying down near the fence, sleeping. I looked at her in the moonlight for a while and thought of her licking me, then I went back in the house. Daddy and Mom were still up. Mom said, "It's almost nine, Abby."

I put my hand on the banister and my foot on the step, and then I just said it. I said, "I want to name the horses. I want to name Blue Jewel 'Sapphire' and Ornery George something nice, like 'Rally.' Black George can stay Black George because it's sort of like a pirate and makes me laugh. I'll think of the others by morning."

I went up the stairs. They didn't say anything, and so I had no idea whether this qualified as sassiness or not. But it did seem as though I had nothing to lose.

The next day was only Tuesday. Imagine that! And then I remembered that we were coming up on spring break, anyway, so I was going to be out of school for a long time. Long enough, I thought, for the school to forget about me completely. Tuesday wasn't bad. Over breakfast, I wrote out the names I had come up with—Jack, Rally, Sapphire, Black George, "Sprinkles" for Roan Jewel, "Sunshine" for Star Jewel, "Webster" for Socks George (I had been stuck for a name, and then my school dictionary was the first thing I laid eyes on when I got up in the morning). I read the names aloud to Mom, and she didn't say that now I was going to get attached to them, she said, "Maybe when we name them, we're really seeing something in them that will help us train them the best way we can."

Maybe. I did like the names. I could see each one in my mind's eye very clearly now. I said, "I think I'm going to get a notebook and write each name on one of the pages, and then I can keep track of things I need to remember about them."

Mom treated me not like she was mad at me, but like she had been mad at me, which was a different thing completely, because Mom always hated getting mad at anyone and felt remorse afterward, so she would make it up in little ways, like giving me a cut-up banana with my Cheerios or opening the apricot jam even though we weren't finished with the strawberry jam. After breakfast, since Daddy was gone into town, she helped me get the horses ready and she let me do Jack first, even though our usual motto was work before pleasure. She stood and watched us, and when he paid attention to me the whole time, keeping his eyes on me and his ears in "learning position"—that is, sort of flopped to either side—she said, "He's learning. You're doing a good job with him." After fifteen minutes of training and some rubbing with the chamois, I put him out with Black George, Rally, and Webster. I watched them for a bit and then went around to each one and patted him and said his name, then gave each of them a piece of carrot. I did the same for the mares, Sapphire, Sprinkles, and Sunshine.

No mention that Daddy had returned from town. In the afternoon, I started with Ornery George—Rally. I went through everything that Jem told me to do—stepping over, stepping back, being sure he was soft through the shoulder, making sure he would turn his head to either side and soften. When he didn't seem quite ready, I got him to run around the pen on his own a bit. Then I walked him to the arena, where I mounted from the fence. I looked at his eye before I got on. He was looking at me, and his eye said, "Who, me?"

Daddy drove in while we were working and came over to the fence. I rode Rally for half an hour, and we did everything Daddy asked us to do, no problem. It was time-consuming, all the steps to getting Rally to do his work without a fuss, but he did it. And I had all the time in the world, didn't I? Afterword, Daddy said, "Abby, you did a very good job on that horse. I'm impressed."

I said, "Rally likes some playtime before his work time."

"Some do," said Daddy.

"But," I said, "you'd better ride him yourself, because if

you're going to tell Mr. Tacker that a grown man can ride him, you'd better be sure."

Daddy frowned as if I were sassing him but then smiled in spite of himself, and I have to say that I laughed as I went into the barn to put away the bridle.

We had a baked chicken for supper, and then I read some of *Julius Caesar*, a play we were reading for English. It wasn't bad. I even stopped looking at the page numbers. Just before I went to bed, Mom came into my room and gave me my new notebook. It was smaller than a school notebook and nicer, too, with heavy green covers. She also gave me a Paper Mate pen—green and silver. She kissed me on the forehead. After she went out, I set them on my desk, and then I put myself to sleep thinking about what I would write in the notebook about each of the horses. The notebook had eighty-eight pages. That was eighty-eight horses. It was fun to think of what I would be writing on the last page.

On Thursday, the only horse we worked in the morning was Rally. I hadn't seen Daddy ride much for several weeks, just because either I was at school or he was making me ride the horses. Now that I had spent so much time with Jem and thinking about Jem, I saw that Daddy was more like Uncle Luke than I had realized, and almost as soon as he began working with Rally, they began arguing. I kept my mouth shut while he was tacking Rally up, even though I thought his brush strokes were too quick and his movements around the horse too brusque. It wasn't that he was doing anything mean, but compared to Jem, he seemed not to think that the horse had any feelings. At first, Rally was his new self, the self I had come to know in the last week or so, paying attention and acting interested. But by the time Daddy was leading Rally to the arena, I saw that Rally's eye was ornery again, and I realized that he was insulted. And maybe that had been the problem all along.

When we got to the arena, Daddy tightened the girth with a jerk, and Rally's ears went back. I said, "I wouldn't get on him just yet if I were you."

"Why not?"

"I would check to see if he's loosened up any or if his back is tight."

"I don't have time. . . ."

"Well, look at his face. He looks a little mad."

"He always looks a little mad."

I went up to Daddy and put my hand on his arm. I looked him in the eye and I said, "No, he doesn't. After Jem started working with him, he stopped looking mad."

"If Jem's training did the trick, then the horse . . ."

"Then it won't be worth the thirty-six dollars we spent if we wreck what he did."

"Are you sassing me, young lady?"

I took a deep breath and then said, "No. I'm being honest and saying what's in my heart."

We looked at each other for a long moment, then he took a deep breath, too, and said, "Well, missy, what do you want me to do?" Now he grinned down at me.

I have to say that I felt a little bossy as I took the rein out of his hand and showed him how to soften Rally by turning his head and his neck, asking him to step back and step over and then go around us in both directions. Then I patted Rally on the face and the neck. I said, "He doesn't like to be treated like a car or something. The others don't mind so much, but he does."

Then Daddy said, "I'm sorry. I guess I wasn't thinking." It sounded like he meant it. He took the rein and did some of the things I had done and then put his foot in the stirrup and got on the horse. It was just about then that Mom came out and checked on us the first time. She was smiling to beat the band but didn't say anything. She passed us and went over to the mares' pasture, where she pretended to do something, then she waved as she went back to the house.

Daddy walked Rally around a little bit and then stopped in front of me. He said, "What now?"

"Well, I would walk him and trot him, changing direction a bunch of times."

I showed him how to lift the inside rein and get the horse to shift his weight and step under. Then I said, "When you're lifting the rein, be sure he steps under right away. Then he won't get lazy and stiff."

Daddy tried this for a few minutes. He was good at it because he could feel the difference in the horse's willingness to do what he was being told between before Rally stepped under and after. Pretty soon he was trying a little of everything—loping, trotting some figure eights, a couple of sliding halts, a long looping gallop around the outside of the arena. Daddy was a good rider the way people are when they learn to ride at an early age and know all the moves without thinking too much about it. Probably most of the horses he had ridden over the years had decided the best thing to do was just go along with him and his ideas, because he was strong and quick and why not let him be the boss? But that didn't work with every horse, as Rally would be the first to tell you.

Mom came out again, just when Daddy was doing some figure eights at the lope, with a change of lead in the middle. She smiled and went back into the house.

I sat on the railing of the arena, looking around our place—at Jack and Black George and the mares, then up at the hawk curving through the blue sky, then over at the house, where purple and white irises were crowding against the porch, then at the dark edges of the mountains across the floor of the valley. Maybe there were a lot of things to wish for, but right then, I couldn't be bothered to wish for anything else than what I saw around me.

Daddy trotted over to me. He said, "I bet we can get at least a thousand for him."

I said, "Mr. Tacker did like him a lot. You could call him and ask how Ruby is doing."

Daddy nodded.

I jumped down off the fence and stroked Rally's nose. Daddy said, "He's a good horse."

I said, "I think he is."

We stood there for a minute, looking at Rally, and then Daddy gave me a squeeze around the shoulders.

Mom came out to check a third time, and I saw that she saw that everything was fine.

After Rally, we did the other horses, but we didn't give them much work—they had done well all week and we expected two good long days Friday and Saturday. By the time we were sitting down to a late lunch of chicken rice soup and ham sandwiches, it seemed like all of us had forgotten about school completely.

Certainly, I had. So, for a moment, I didn't even recognize Gloria's mom's car when it pulled up behind the truck. Then Gloria threw open the door and jumped out shouting, "Abby! Abby! Wait till you hear!"

Mom opened the door, and Gloria ran in and hugged me. I said, "Hear what?" I remembered the way her face went blank when she saw the necklace in my locker on Monday, and I decided I wasn't going to fall for just any old story. But it was hard to resist how she was now—jumping up and down and grinning. She exclaimed, "Kyle came back!"

"Kyle came back from where? Kyle Gonzalez?" I sounded a little doubtful, I know. But Kyle?

"Yes! He saved you!"

"Where was he?"

"He was home sick! He had pinkeye or something gross like that, so he was out Friday, Monday, and Tuesday. And you know no one talks to him much, so when he got back yesterday, he didn't know what happened to you until the end of the day, and then he told!"

Mom asked Gloria's mom to sit down and have a cup of coffee or tea, and she did, but Gloria was just jumping around the table, she was so excited. Daddy said, "Gloria, what did he tell?"

Gloria's mom said, "Settle down, Glow. One thing at a time!"

But she didn't settle down. She exclaimed, "He was fixing the bells! He was fixing the bells on your mission so they would ring better or something, and when he stood up, he saw her pick up the necklace off the floor!"

"Who?"

"Stella. It was Stella who found the necklace on the floor

228

of the lunchroom, and then, *she said,* she was coming out of the lunchroom to turn it in, and she saw that it belonged to Joan, and so she was afraid to do anything with it because of the anonymous note."

Gloria's mom said, "What anonymous note?"

"Well, it's not anonymous anymore. Debbie admitted that she sent it."

I said, "Debbie!"

"Yes! Debbie saw Stella put the ink cartridge on Joan's chair and she thought Joan should know, but she was afraid of Stella."

"You should never do anything anonymously—" began Mrs. Harris.

"Stella didn't see Debbie—she's so quiet. But she knew *you* had been sitting behind her, so she thought you—"

"Abby would never send an anonymous note!" exclaimed Mom. "Would you?"

"I did see it," I said.

"You should have come forward," said Mom.

But Gloria rushed on, so I didn't have to answer her. "She kept the necklace all day Thursday and all day Friday, and she was scared to death the whole time, because Mr. Canning was so mad and talking about the police, so—"

"So—"

She sat down and leaned toward me as if she was telling the punch line. "So, *she said,* she waited until the end of school, after the bus left Friday, and she pushed it through the air vents of your locker."

"Why my locker?"

"Well, *she said,* she was trying to get it into that empty

locker near yours, but she miscounted and pushed it through your vents instead."

Mom said, "Is there an empty locker near yours, Abby?"

"Mine is six from the end of that row, and the fourth one is the empty one."

"Is it locked?" said Daddy.

"They're all locked," said Gloria. "But she was mad about the anonymous note. I think she knew perfectly well that it was your locker."

Mom and Mrs. Harris shook their heads.

Daddy said, "Why didn't Kyle come forward last week?"

"Why does Kyle do anything?" said Gloria. "He said that he didn't think the necklace was any big deal on Thursday, but then when he found out that you got blamed, he had to tell."

"That sounds like Kyle," I said. "He did a good job on our mission." I glanced at Daddy. "He doesn't do anything if he can't do it right."

"Well," said Daddy. "That's a virtue in anyone."

Now Gloria sat down in a chair beside me and put her elbows on the table and her chin in her hands, staring at me. She said, "So, you're going to come to school tomorrow, right?" She looked like she always had, just Gloria, my friend. I decided I was wrong about that other look I thought I'd seen. She grinned. I grinned back at her.

Mom said, "We haven't heard anything from Mr. Canning, Gloria."

"I'm still suspended."

And then the phone rang. It was Mr. Canning, unsuspending me.

* * *

In the end, I didn't go back to school the next day, since vacation was almost here and nothing much was going on anyway, but over the weekend, Gloria brought me my assignments, and we worked on them together. When you are suspended, you can't do that work, and so you get Fs on it, so for once I was relieved to have homework.

On Monday, Mr. Tacker came by, and on Wednesday, he brought his trailer to take Rally away to his ranch. He said he would get Jem Jarrow to help prepare Rally for the big summer parade. He paid Daddy a thousand dollars, and Daddy gave me fifty for myself. Mom took me to town and we opened a savings account. Mr. Tacker said he would keep his name, Rally. I said I would come to the parade and watch him.

On Tuesday, Stella called and said that she was really sorry and that she hoped I would forgive her and still be her friend. She had learned her lesson. I said, "What lesson?" I'm sure I sounded grumpy.

Stella sounded, as Mom would have said, "truly repentant." She said, "Well, lots of them. Way too many. I guess—" There was a long pause. "I guess the main one is, well, I don't want to be mean, really. I get mean sort of not really intending to, but I know I shouldn't be mean. I have a mean thought, and then I get carried away. I guess the main lesson is not to get carried away. Don't you know what I'm talking about? Something you shouldn't say comes into your head and you just say it, even though you know you shouldn't?"

I told her I knew what she was talking about. I still wondered if she had pushed that necklace through my locker vents on purpose, but it seemed mean, as long as we were talking about being mean, to ask.

I told her I would still be her friend.

She said, "Thank you, Abby."

It sounded like she meant it. What I meant, I have to admit, was We'll see. But I decided that was a private thought.

On Wednesday, Miss Slater called and said that she had entered me and Gallant Man in four classes in the spring show; would I come out Saturday and sit on him for an hour or so? That night, I had a little free time, so I sat down with my notebook and wrote the names in my best handwriting. Under the name Rally, I wrote everything I had learned about him, and then, at the bottom, I wrote, *A little girl can ride him.*

About the Author

Jane Smiley is the author of many books for adults, including *Horse Heaven*, *Moo*, and the Pulitzer Prize–winning *A Thousand Acres*. She was inducted into the American Academy of Arts and Letters in 2001.

Jane Smiley lives in Northern California, where she rides horses every chance she gets. *The Georges and the Jewels* is her first novel for young readers.